REDEMPTION IN THE WILDERNESS

FRONTIER HEARTS
BOOK TWO

ANDREA BYRD

ISBN-13: 978-1-942265-79-5

CHAPTER 1

May 28, 1780
Green County, Kentucky

Margaret Blair's heart pounded in her ears as she aimed her father's rifle. Careful not to bite the inside of her jaw as she had done the time before, she clenched her teeth instead, her arms quivering under the weight of the weapon. With a single swallow, she pulled the trigger. A ringing exploded in her ears as she tumbled backward a step. Her target leapt through the meadow away from her, his white tail waving like a warning flag to any other deer in the area. A groan slipped from Margaret's body as her shoulders sagged. Not again.

At the rate she was going, she and Muireall would starve before spring was up. Margaret shook her head and turned to begin the trek back down into the valley where her family's cabin stood. A red-breasted robin flitted from one tree branch to another, then cocked his head in her direction. Margaret sighed. Not a single creature in the Kentucky countryside found her to be a threat.

Without trying to disguise her presence after the failed hunt, she trudged back toward the cabin. Twigs snapped underfoot and fern fronds rustled as she brushed past them. A gray squirrel scampered up the nearest oak and scurried around to the backside when she came up on him. His barking chatter mocked her as she passed before she entered a bright clearing in the trees. The sun beat down upon her back, hinting at the coming summer.

At the snap of a branch behind her, Margaret whirled around. As she scanned for danger, her pulse quickened. Anxiety rippled through her chest and climbed up the back of her neck. She spotted nothing save the endless varieties of trees and plants.

A loud, quick hammering sounded from the other direction. She spun once more, afraid her heart would simply give out as it continued its reckless pounding. But she quickly located the source of this new noise. A red-capped woodpecker hammered on the tree to her left. Margaret allowed the breath to rush from her body. She paused only a moment to watch his rapid pecking before she resumed her course. Her pace carried an extra fervor. The sensation of being watched was too strong to deny, as it had been many times lately.

By the time she reached the cabin her father had built into a hillside, her breaths had become labored from exertion. Stopping on the porch that spanned the entire length of the house, Margaret stood with her hand on the door. Closing her eyes, she concentrated on stuffing her concern deep within the depths of her mind where it had no control over her pulse. Then, once her mind had settled sufficiently and her breaths slowed, she pressed a hand to the door. Her shoulders dropped when it did not budge.

"Muireall." She bellowed out the groan through the wooden door, her foot tapping out a quick rhythm on the porch as she waited. She glanced back toward the tree line, scanning the shadows.

A shuffling sounded inside before she heard the bar being lifted from its place. Finally, Muireall's pale, innocent face peeped through the door. Margaret raised her brow and pressed her lips together. "Ye can see 'tis only me." She did her best to keep her voice level. Though her sister's caution was understandable, the extent of it bordered on illogical these days.

Muireall gave her an apologetic grin. "Ye know it makes me nervous when ye are away."

Margaret released a sigh as her younger sister darted back over to the hearthside rocking chair and retrieved her embroidery from its seat. "I know," she replied, but Muireall's attention was already diverted to the fabric and thread. Margaret crossed her arms. She waited a moment to see if her sister would ask about the hunt before she added, "I hate to disappoint ye, me darlin' sister, but once again, me huntin' trip has proved in vain."

"Oh. Well, ye know I would rather not deal with the meat, anyhow." Muireall glanced up from her embroidery only long enough to wave a hand.

Margaret frowned. If she had brought down a deer, Muireall would not have lifted a finger to aid in the butchering. Instead, she would have remained where she was now, consumed in the very same task. "Well, I suppose t'will be boiled potatoes again tonight."

That drew Muireall's attention. "Aww, I am so tired of boiled potatoes." Her voice came out as a petulant whine as she peered at Margaret through long, dark lashes. A frown curved her perfectly pink lips downward. "Why can we not have somethin' else?"

"Because we have nothin' else." The words came out tighter

than Margaret meant them, so she smiled and added, "At least we have those wild onions to add to it now."

Muireall made a face and, honestly, she could not blame the girl. Though Margaret was glad to add a different flavor to the otherwise tasteless dish, her boiled potatoes with wild onions was not the most appetizing meal. Mulberries, however, were a favorite of her sister's.

"But the mulberries are ripening up nicely. Would ye want to help me with the harvest tomorrow?"

Muireall's gaze flitted to the door and back again. Even across the room, Margaret could see the tears swimming in the seventeen-year-old's eyes. The past three months, since their mither passed only two months after their father, had been difficult on her sister. More and more, she had retreated into herself.

Margaret crossed the space and kneeled before her, placing a hand on her wrist. "Come on," she urged. "They are yer favorite."

She met Muireall's dark-blue eyes, which were so beautifully set in a porcelain face and framed with hair as black as a raven. But today, those eyes held a fear and sadness that cut Margaret to her core. Her thumb worked back and forth over the soft flesh of her sister's wrist as she made her silent plea.

Finally, a small smile eased the tension in Muireall's face, and her head dipped in a nod.

"Good." Hope sprung in Margaret's heart like the first shoot of a flower poking through the soil in spring. Since their mother passed, Muireall had set foot outside only when absolutely necessary. Otherwise, she clung to the imagined safety of the cabin.

Margaret knew better, though—nowhere was truly safe. Though their father had died in a tragic accident outside the cabin, their mither had died right there in her bed of the ague.

As she stood, her gaze flicked to the bed that had not been slept in since the day she buried her mither.

After their parents' passing, the spring had brought Indian raids. Led by the British, Shawnee had put the entire area on edge as they claimed countless lives. The smell of the Pucketts' burning cabin still filled her nose as she recalled the black smoke billowing through the air while she stood on the ridge. She had gone to see if she could join the men on their next hunt but was met with devastation instead. Why their own cabin had been spared when they only lived over the ridge and down the valley, she would never know. But she would also be forever grateful.

For Margaret, the troubled times only reassured the belief that it was best to live one's life to the fullest, to experience all God offered. For life could be gone in the blink of an eye. But Muireall, five years younger than her own twenty-two, had become a recluse, timid as a field mouse.

"I will go an' fetch those potatoes, then." Margaret smiled for her sister's sake. But Muireall nodded without looking up from the white fabric she dipped her needle in and out of.

With a sigh, Margaret ducked back outdoors. Her boots echoed against the wooden porch as she headed toward the little barn they used mostly as a storehouse. Nearing the wood-pile, she stopped. Her brows pulled together and her head tilted to the side. Just the night before, she had noted how it had dwindled to nearly nothing. But with only using the wood for cooking, they could have made it another day or two before she chopped more. Now, though, the small pile was three logs high across its entirety.

Fear prickled up her spine and into her hairline. Turning in a slow circle, she carefully scanned the valley. Her breaths came fast and shallow, her chest heaving as she checked over every tree and bush twice. Once again, she could not shake the feeling that she was not alone.

~

he morning after the brunette's failed hunt, Iain Donegal laid on his stomach at the edge of a ridge under cover of a broad pine. The roots poked unevenly into his midsection and limbs, but the soft dirt and inviting shade made for an excellent place to wait for the women to emerge from the cabin below. Normally, he held off until they slept to provide aid, doing just enough to keep them on their feet but little enough to go unnoticed. But the rabbit could not be left overnight. There was too large a chance for scavengers to steal the precious meat.

Though, it might take a miracle for him to catch both of the women away from the cabin long enough to make his drop. The younger, darker-headed of the two did not seem to leave but once in a blue moon. However, it would not be the first miracle Iain had witnessed over the course of the past year. His own life was a testament to that. Despite the ear missing from the right side of his head, his had been one of only three lives spared in a Chickamauga raid the previous winter.

Iain would never understand why his own worthless life had been allowed to continue while so many innocents died. For the past several years, he had taken to the wilds of Kentucky and avoided connections, for he held no esteem for his own existence. And yet, the Lord continually protected him. Iain's mouth pulled into a frown as he stared down at the rough-hewn cabin in the valley below.

A tiny voice within him said that it was because God had a plan for him, but Iain pushed the thought away. Still, as he waited, his thoughts drifted to the moment that had kept him tethered in one location much longer than he had ever planned. As he had roamed the hills of Kentucky hunting and gathering hides, he had stumbled upon the older of the two sisters burying her mother. Staying hidden, Iain had watched as she tearfully rolled the sheet-wrapped body into the shallow grave and covered it with dirt. In that moment, something had wrenched within his chest, and an unbidden connection had been forged.

No matter how he attempted to convince himself it was of no concern to him, Iain had not been able to move on as he had intended. Later that night, he had crept close and read the names carved into the simple crosses the woman had placed at the head of the grave and the still relatively fresh one beside it. Malcom and Iona, her parents, he presumed. And considering she had dug the second grave herself, that meant there was no brother to lead the household. No one to take care of her, and later, he learned, her sister.

Since then, some guiding hand or deep-seated sense of duty had kept Iain nearby. Keeping an eye on them, he had quickly learned the older daughter was a terrible shot. Despite her countless, well-meant attempts at hunting, he still was not sure she could hit the broad side of a barn should she try. So now, after her latest non-success, he waited patiently to leave a rabbit from his snares on their porch. Their food stores were swindling, and he was not confident they would survive without further intervention.

Finally, Iain's prayers were answered. The brunette emerged from the cabin, her arms laden with a sheet and baskets, her younger sister on her tail. The younger girl appeared pale from her time indoors, and her eyes darted nervously about as she stayed close on her sister's heels. Together, they climbed the hillside the cabin was built into and disappeared over the opposite ridge.

Once they had been gone a sufficient amount of time, he collected his mare from where she grazed down the hill from his perch. Before he mounted, he paused beside a cedar and used his knife to remove a couple of small branches. The prickly needles poked at his skin and shirtsleeves as he worked, and their fragrance filled his nose.

Then, slipping onto the mare's bare back, Iain guided her over the ridge and down the hillside to the cabin. At the porch, he dismounted and placed the dead rabbit near the door, covered in the only remaining handkerchief in his care. He gathered four decent-sized rocks to place at each corner to weight the fabric down and laid the cedar branches overtop to mask the scent. Frowning down at the pile, he sent a prayer up that no varmints would touch it before the women found it.

Though the prayer likely bounced off the scarce clouds above, it made Iain feel better for abandoning the precious meat to follow the women. But he could not, in good conscience, allow them to go traipsing off alone in the Kentucky wilderness without keeping an eye on them. Far too many dangers lurked around every bend. So he remounted and nudged the golden mare toward the hillside behind the cabin. Fortunately, their path was easy to follow, and he quickly located them in a valley near where the older sister had hunted the day before. An abundance of mulberry trees lined the valley, laden with red and purple berries.

After locating a place for the mare to graze contentedly out of sight, Iain crouched in hiding. As he scanned the land below, his heart leapt into his throat. Where was the older sister? A plain white sheet was spread below a mulberry tree, and the younger sister stood, staring wide-eyed into the tree above. Iain's brows pulled together. Was she in the tree? A second later, the branches on one side of the tree began to shake, and ripe mulberries fell to the sheet in droves. Then, suddenly, the brunette was shimmying back down from the tree like an agile little bobcat.

He averted his gaze as her petticoats caught in a branch and lifted to reveal her stockings. But the next moment, she had both feet back on the ground with her decency returned. Then she instructed her sister as they lifted the edges of the sheet and guided the mulberries into the center, from where they were easily gathered into baskets. After the berries were collected, the sheet, now speckled with mulberry juices, was moved to the other side of the tree. And the brunette went scurrying up into the tree's branches once more.

The corner of his mouth tipped up as he watched her scale the tree as though it was nothing. Though the woman's appearance was not noteworthy, her hair the same drab brown as the dirt under the pine he had hidden behind that morning, there was a quality about her that drew him. If he weren't no good, he would be tempted to reveal himself to her, to offer to be the man in her life. But that could never be. He could never have those kinds of ties.

⁓

Though Margaret's muscles were tired, her heart and baskets were full. She might fail as a hunter, but at least they had harvested enough mulberries to get through for a short while. And she had been blessed to do so alongside her sister.

Muireall darted a glance behind her at Margaret as they topped the hill leading down into the valley they called home. Margaret smiled at the girl, whose cheeks had taken on a pink tint throughout the long morning. Though her dark-blue eyes still had a healthy dose of fear swimming in them, her face held a glow that had not been there for months. Margaret could not ask for more as she carefully made her way down the hillside. Watching her sister's dark skirt, she followed her steps as they approached the cabin, picking their way over the thick green grass.

But when Muireall stepped onto the wooden porch, she stopped in her tracks. Margaret nearly plowed into her back and halted just short of spilling her overloaded baskets. "What is it?"

Muireall backed up, pointing down the length of the porch, her face drained of color. Margaret's brows furrowed as she was forced to take a step aside. But then her gaze followed her sister's pointing finger. When she beheld the strange mound near the door, her heart quickened. Margaret slowly settled the baskets and the stained sheet on the edge of the porch before she approached.

She knelt, and with shaking hands, lifted fragrant cedar branches to reveal a white square beneath. Margaret closed her eyes and took a deep breath before raising the fabric to reveal what was beneath. Her heart pounded in her chest as she stared down at a dead rabbit.

Such a blessing, and yet, it sent her reeling into a world of fear. Her gaze snapped to the hillside. Though her search revealed nothing, she could be certain now. They were not alone.

CHAPTER 2

argaret frowned down at her mulberry jam as she scraped the long spoon against the bottom of the pot. The stench of charred berries reached her nose, and coughs sputtered from her chest. Smoke swirled in the air, intermingling with the already strange smell of both sweet and burnt berries. She groaned before she hoisted herself from where she knelt on the ground and hurried the pot over to the table, where she settled it on a folded towel. The reddish-purple mush bubbled and boiled, splattering its contents at her as pockets of air rose up and out of its depths.

From the end of the table, Muireall lifted judgmental eyes, her lips pulled into a tight little purse. Her pale, thin hand hovered over her embroidery, and her dark eyebrows arched in Margaret's direction. "Did ye ruin the last of our sugar?"

Guilt and frustration seeped through Margaret in equal portions, heating her neck and face. She pressed her own lips together to hold in the snide remark that threatened to spill from her. Instead, she stared down into the charred jam and settled the towels she had used to carry it onto the table. Though her sister's actions made her want to scream at times, it was not completely Muireall's fault that she now casted judgment instead of lifting a finger to aid in the cooking or housekeeping. How many times had she been asked to scrub the floor while Ma and Muireall stitched clothing with one another, only to have their mither find some fault in her work when she was done? "Nay," she replied tightly, as though saying it would make it so.

Whipping a towel from the table, she turned and stalked back to the fireplace. Gathering several of the jars that had been warming by the fire, she moved them to the table and filled them with her jam. *Lord, please dinnae let it be as bad as it smells.* The corners of her mouth turned down as she tightened the lids onto the jars, praying they would seal properly.

Once Margaret had filled their short supply of jars, she scraped the remaining jam into a bowl. "Ye want to try some on toast?" She glanced in Muireall's direction.

Her sister lifted a shoulder but not her gaze. Margaret rolled her eyes and turned to the shelf where the remnants of a loaf of bread sat. The last loaf of bread until they could obtain more flour...

Unease swirled in her stomach, but she gripped the handle of the knife tighter and cut two slices away from the hard loaf. Thus far, her attempts at bread-making had been about as successful as the jam. This loaf in her hands had been no exception. The crusty exterior was a dark, bitter-tasting brown. Still, she placed a rack over the fire and settled the two slices atop it to warm for a moment. Though it might not be the treat it had been while they were growing up, the toast and jam was still a blessing.

Margaret stood and swiped her arm across her forehead to clear the sweat from her brow. With a fire crackling on the warm May day, the cabin had transformed into a roasting oven, and her clothing was drenched with sweat. Waving a hand to cool her face, she stalked over and unbarred the door. Swinging it open, she used the same large, sand-colored rock their mother had used to prop open the door.

"Ah." Margaret closed her eyes and breathed deeply of the fresh air that filtered in through the doorway. She relished the gentle sweep of the breeze against her flaming cheeks.

"What do ye think ye are doin'?"

Muireall's cry startled her from her moment of peace and sent her whirling in her sister's direction. The girl had finally risen from her chair and stood staring incredulously at the open door.

"I was burnin' up," Margaret retorted as she took a step toward her. "Ma always opened the door when she cooked in the summer."

Muireall's face turned a deep shade of red, and tears popped into her eyes, making Margaret immediately regret her choice of words. "Ma is not here anymore." Her sister forced the words through tight lips, the tears spilling down her cheeks. Her whole body shook with emotion.

"I know. I am sorry." Margaret rushed to her and wrapped her arms around her.

Though Muireall did not return her embrace, she did not push her away. Her sister's body convulsed as sobs racked her body. Margaret closed her eyes tightly against the tears that threatened. Her mither's words right before her death came flooding back to her, and bile rose at the back of her throat. *Dinnae let her die out here like the rest of us.* Would she be able to hold to her promise? Or would they both wither away here in the Kentucky wilderness? *Nay, Lord, I cannae let that happen. Please provide a way, Lord.* Margaret squeezed Muireall tighter.

A sudden thud behind her caused her to whirl away from her sister. Muireall's sniffles came to a sudden stop, but the sound was replaced with Margaret's heart pounding in her ears. Her eyes widened as she took in the massive silhouette of a man standing in the open doorway. Instinctively, she held a hand out in front of Muireall and took a half step in front of her. More thumps sounded on the wooden porch, causing her breaths to become erratic. Dread sliced through her. He was not alone.

Margaret swallowed down the scream that rose in her throat as the man stepped into the cabin. As he moved out of the bright light, she took in his haggard and unwashed appearance. He licked his tongue over rotting teeth as he drew closer, an evil glint in his exceptionally dark eyes. "He-eh-eh. Look what we have here, Randall. Not only did we find us a cabin, but after all these days a travelin' with not a woman in sight, here is two purty ones just a waitin' for us." His gaze slid over Margaret's body, making her want to squirm, but instead, she lifted her chin.

As the second man moved into view, she sent a quick glance in his direction. Though he was not as tall or broad as the first, the gleam in his green eyes held a nefarious intent that sent a prickle up her spine. "Our pa will be back directly."

A low, deep chuckle came from the first man. The hoarse sound rasped against her ears and chilled her to the bone. "That not yer daddy's grave out beside the cabin?"

Margaret swallowed again, suddenly wishing she had found a place away from their home to bury their parents. But she was not strong enough to carry a body farther. Just as she would not be strong enough to fend off these men. *Lord, please send help.* She sent the desperate prayer up before she lifted her chin again. "Nay. That was our brother."

The men shared a sinister look before they erupted in raucous laughter that made her flinch. The massive man stepped within a foot of her, his stench curling her nose. Muireall's fingers wrapped tightly around her forearm. "This one has got some spirit, for sure," he drawled. "But I want that one."

"No!" She and Muireall both screamed as he pushed past Margaret and moved toward Muireall. Margaret lunged for him, but he sent her reeling with one swift backhand. Her body slammed into the thick wooden table, and his gaze never even left Muireall. Pain erupted in Margaret's hip before she fell to the floor.

Vile laughter filled her ears, along with Muireall's screams as he seized her. Margaret grabbed for the man's leg as he passed, Muireall thrown over his shoulder. She wrapped her hands around the thick limb and dug into the grimy material of his breeches. But again, he flicked her away like a fly. This time, she took a boot to the face. Margaret rolled away, blinking as her world turned black.

When her vision returned, the blond man's laughing face loomed before her. A silent scream tore up through her throat. But it did not stop him from moving his body over hers. Margaret kicked furiously with both legs. When, finally, she landed a kick that sent him reeling backward—clutching his nether regions in pain, a string of vile curses slipping from his mouth—Margaret did not stick around to listen. Instead, she crawled away, trying to regain her footing, to reach their parent's bed, where her sister's tormented screams were being muffled.

A searing-hot pain tore through her calf, and she cried out, dropping to the floor. She reached toward the injury but stopped as a wave of nausea and dizziness washed over her. A metal blade stuck from her leg. The hilt protruded from one side while the point poked from the other. It was all Margaret could do to hold onto reality. When the man stood over her with a hungry gleam in his eyes, she almost wished to succumb to the black world that called her. But she could not stop fighting. For Muireall's sake.

A shot rang through the cabin, and the man's face changed. Blood seeped from his mouth as the life drained from his eyes. Margaret attempted to scramble backward as he fell forward, but he crashed on top of her, flattening her to the ground. Tears sprang to her eyes in relief that the man would not be able to accomplish the terrible task he had set upon. But with his reeking, unwashed body across hers, her stomach roiled.

Sounds of struggle came to her where she laid pinned under the blond man's body, the pain in her leg pulsing and searing. With effort, she pushed him from atop her. Heat coursed through her from the exertion, but she had to press on. She needed to get to Muireall. Her gaze flew to the bed where sister's thin body lay, her skirts pulled up around her knees and splayed all around. The sounds of her whimpering tore Margaret's heart out.

"Muir—" She made to get up, but pain stopped her short. Trying again, she drug herself over a straight-backed chair and gripped the side. But when she pressed her weight against the side of the seat, the chair toppled over atop her. Hot tears sprang into her eyes. "Muireall," she cried.

On the other side of the bed, a person stood up. Margaret's heart kicked up a notch before she noticed it was not one of their assailants. Instead, it was a tall, thin man with hair as black as night. His gaze caressed Muireall's body in a much different way than those of the two previous men had. He bent and whispered something to her. Though Muireall shook her head and did not attempt to move away, her whimpering cries wrenched through Margaret's chest. But the man backed away, his mouth pressed into a line.

His gaze lifted to Margaret's. Her breath caught as his sky-blue eyes found hers. Even from across the room, she could tell they were filled with compassion. The storm that brewed across his features was not one of malicious intent, but of concern.

*I*ain cast one last glance at the man lying on the floor beside him, but the grayish pallor of the assailant's skin told Iain he would no longer be a nuisance. A cold chill passed over his body, but he ignored it, reassuring himself that he had done what had to be done. The younger sister's honor was barely intact as it was. Though she had shaken her head when he asked if she was injured, she now lay crying into the pillow. He could only imagine how deeply her mental wounds ran. But, convinced she was not physically harmed, he turned his attention to the brunette.

Despite whatever injuries she had sustained, her eyes were alert as she met his gaze without fear. Quickly, but cautiously, he moved around the end of the bed and made his way across the room to her. Her attention never left his face as he approached and knelt before her. His heart pounded in his chest, as much a lasting effect of the fight as from her nearness.

Avoiding her scrutiny, Iain turned his focus to removing the chair atop her. After righting it, he frowned at the blade sticking through her calf and the blood-stained stocking still covering her leg. He swallowed and his brows pulled together. "Are ye hurt anywhere else?"

When he lifted his face to hers again, her face was already turning an angry shade of purple. Her gaze was not fixed on his face, though, but on the right side of his head. Iain's hand flew to the spot where his ear was missing, leaving an ugly hole and unsightly scars. He must have lost his hat in the fight. He cleared his throat. "Old injury," he muttered.

Her eyes snapped to his then, and she seemed to remember his question. She started to shake her head but stopped. Closing her eyes as she wavered, she pressed a hand to her temple. "Me head," she breathed as she pried her lids open under a scrunched brow. "But me leg is worse."

Iain nodded, his heart skipping a beat at the familiar accent whispered in a woman's voice. "I need to move ye over to the bed."

The brunette returned his nod, and he moved in beside her, slipping an arm under her legs and behind her back. Her breathing hitched, but she made no other indication of the pain he must be causing her. Even in the middle of such a dire situation, her strength astounded him. But likely, he would find the limits of her strength before the ordeal was over. His mouth pressed tight as he settled her onto the bed beside her sister.

"Muireall." She reached out to brush at her sister's dark hair.

The younger woman pulled her face from the pillow but watched him warily. Though he could understand her mistrust, he needed her assistance.

"Can ye help me attend to yer sister?" He raised his brows in question. Her deep-blue eyes darted to the older girl.

"Please." The brunette nodded her encouragement.

Muireall hesitated before she slowly got up from the bed. Iain's heart ached to ask anything of her. The girl would bear emotional scars from this day, but unlike her sister, she had come through the ordeal physically unharmed, and it was time to help.

He cleared his throat. "I need needle an' thread. Hot water 'n' towels. An' did yer pa keep any strong drink around the house?"

The brunette lifted a trembling arm. "Bottom shelf, in the corner."

Iain frowned at the hoarseness that had seeped into her voice. Her strength was fading. "I will get it," he advised, placing a hand on her arm.

He strode across the room and retrieved the bottle hidden in the back corner of the bottom shelf. Then he grabbed a chair from the table and returned to the brunette's side. A moment later, her sister brought the other supplies and went to heat the water.

Suddenly, Iain hesitated to begin the task at hand. He looked up into the woman's face as she watched him. He searched her eyes and found there an ocean of both color and emotion. This was not the kind of woman who shied away from what had to be done.

"This will hurt."

She gave a nod before she closed those beautiful eyes.

Iain took a deep breath, then pulled the blade from her leg. A whimper escaped her, but he ignored it as he used the same blade to cut the stocking away from the bottom portion of her leg. Her skin was milky white except for the thick line of marred flesh with red shining beneath. Uncorking the bottle that held barely a swig of rum, he poured it inside. This time, a gasp turned into a scream, and thankfully, the woman fainted. For the longest—and possibly most difficult—part was about to begin. Iain threaded the white thread through the needle and lowered it to her soft flesh.

Swallowing, he closed his eyes and offered up a prayer. *Lord, please be with her. Please let her pull through.* And then, with everything in him, he hoped the Lord actually heard and heeded his prayer.

~

*M*argaret opened her eyes to a cabin that was dark aside from the dim light of the crackling fire. For one blissful moment, she was perfectly content. That was, before her leg twitched, sending a shock of pain that nearly made her cry out. As she clamped her mouth shut, the events of the day came flooding back to her. Immediately, she sought Muireall out. A relieved breath whooshed out of her lungs as she laid eyes on her younger sister, curled next to her, sleeping peacefully. Carefully, she brushed a lock of silky black hair from Muireall's soft, creamy skin.

Thank Ye, Lord, for keeping her safe.

Despite the trials of the day and the aches and pains that were making themselves known, she was entirely grateful that they had come through no worse for wear. Thanks to their mysterious defender who had shown up just in the nick of time. Margaret's brows pulled together as she glanced around. Had he disappeared as quickly as he arrived? A cold chill traveled up her spine.

But her eyes lighted upon the dark-haired stranger near the fire. He must have noticed her stirring, for he poured a cup of hot liquid from the kettle and brought it to her. "Here, drink this. 'Tis feverfew tea, an' 'twill help with the pain."

His deep, raspy voice was an odd comfort, considering she had yet to learn his name. She accepted the cup and blew on the steaming liquid. Venturing a glance at his profile in the firelight, with his jawline covered in a five o'clock shadow, she broached the question on her mind. "Who are ye?"

He turned his light-blue eyes upon her, but his mouth pressed into a thin line. His Adam's apple bobbed before he answered. "Iain Donegal." His gaze roamed over her face as she sipped the strange new tea.

Though she knew of the feverfew plant and its cheery blooms that came later in the summer, she had never had a brew from its leaves. The taste, as it splashed over her tongue, was a pleasant surprise compared to their fare of late. But another question burned at her, leaving an unease that swirled in her stomach with the drink. "An' how did ye come to find us?"

Mr. Donegal's mouth pressed thinner. "I am a long hunter."

Was that the full truth? His eyes did not shift from hers, but something within their depths told her there was more to his story. Such as how he had come upon them at the exact moment he had. But as her pain lessened, sleep tugged at her once more. The rest of the story would have to wait until morning.

Lord, please watch over us until we can learn more of this man.

"Can I ask yer name?" The question pulled her back to the present as the cup was lifted from her fingers.

"Margaret Blair," she whispered. "An' me sister is Muireall."

CHAPTER 3

A prodding at her shoulder pulled Margaret from the world of slumber. Forcing her swollen eyelids to part, she found Muireall staring at her wide-eyed. The girl motioned to where Mr. Donegal leaned over the fire, frying something in a pan. Margaret closed her eyes as she inhaled the delicious aroma, and her stomach gurgled in response. Peering back at Muireall, she smiled and covered her sister's hand with hers. "Dinnae fash yerself. He is a long hunter."

Muireall gazed at her warily before she eased from the bed. Gathering a shawl over her shoulders, she slipped from the cabin, presumably to attend to morning matters.

Margaret pulled herself into a sitting position and winced at the pain in both her hip and leg. She would have to enlist Muireall's help to attend to her own daily needs. Her mouth pulled into a frown before a clanking by the fire drew her attention back to Mr. Donegal's long, lean form.

Having moved the food onto plates, he settled one on the table and brought two in her direction. Margaret's eyes widened at the sight of a warm meal complete with meat and eggs. Her mouth watered in anticipation. Mr. Donegal laid a plate and fork onto her lap before he sat in the chair next to the bed.

"Thank ye kindly, Mr. Donegal." She dipped her head in thanks. "This is…" Margaret stopped to keep from divulging that they had not had such sustenance in a quite some time.

The man did not look up from his plate when he replied. "'Tis nothin'. Quail eggs 'n' some jerked venison." He shoveled his own eggs into his mouth before he glanced at the closed door. "Didna think yer sister would be up to fixin' anythin' this mornin'."

Margaret pursed her lips as she glanced at her sister's plate waiting on the table. Muireall had not prepared a meal a day in her life. Was their situation so easily read? Though that thought was concerning, a more urgent one regarding the man seated at her side tugged at her. Her brows pulled together, but she took another bite of eggs before she turned back to him. "Ye said ye were a long hunter?"

He nodded—a slow, measured movement.

"How did ye come to be here in this valley right when we needed ye?"

His eyes snapped up to hers, and suddenly, she wished she could recall the question. Those light-blue depths seemed to have turned to ice. He hesitated, and Margaret's heart beat harder as their gazes remained locked together.

But the door opened, drawing their attention as Muireall slipped inside. Her eyes were wide and her breathing fast as she pressed her body against the door. "Reverend Graham is coming down the hill."

Margaret sat up straighter, and Donegal bolted to his feet. What would the man think if he saw them in such a state? What would he think of a strange man in their home? She swallowed. Loosening her hair, she dashed her fingers through it and re-braided it. Still leaning against the door, Muireall did the same, then did her best to smooth her rumpled dress from the day before. Margaret glanced at Mr. Donegal. "Help me to a chair."

He lifted a brow. "I will help ye if ye wish. But I dinnae think ye will be able to hide the entire ordeal from him."

Margaret tilted her head in question before he nodded at her face. Her lips parted as she reached up, remembering how puffy her eyes had felt when she first awoke. As she gently touched her face, her swollen and undoubtedly bruised skin gave evidence of the backhand and kick. How would they ever explain? Would Reverend Graham believe it if they told him the truth? Or would he think Mr. Donegal was to blame? Only one way to find out.

She lifted her chin. "Help me to a chair, anyway."

The corner of Donegal's mouth twitched as though he might smile. Instead, he stood and came to place an arm around her shoulders. Margaret leaned into his strength as she limped across the room to a chair, careful not to put weight on her injured leg. Though her ribs and side protested the movement, it was nice to trust in the support of a man and feel his sturdy frame so close against hers. She'd had to carry the load of the family for so many endless months. And even before then, her father had never truly been someone she could lean on.

In fact, the feel of Mr. Donegal, his muscles moving under her hand where she gripped his shirt and his strong hand at her waist, was completely foreign. One that was delightfully wonderful. To her, it served as a reminder of how God had made man and woman for one another.

As soon as she settled into the straight-back chair, Reverend Graham's knock came at the door. Ignoring the pulsing pain in her leg, Margaret straightened her posture and forced a smile as Muireall swung the door open.

Reverend Graham gave them a broad, toothy grin, his dark hair ruffled and his hat in his hand. "Good mornin', ladies.

Thought I would stop in to see how you were farin', but it appears I am not the first to do so." He gave a short bow before he strode across the room and offered a hand to Mr. Donegal, who stood protectively by Margaret's chair. "Reverend Robert Graham. Glad to make your acquaintance." He smiled up at the stranger who dwarfed him in size.

"Iain Donegal," the man at her shoulder said, his tone unreadable.

"And how are—" Reverend Graham stopped mid-sentence as he turned to Margaret. "What has happened to you, my child?"

Though the man was not likely old enough to be her father, she smiled at the endearment. While he rarely made it out their way, he was nothing if not cordial and caring every time. The perfect personality for the head of a church, she always thought.

But Margaret hesitated, convincing herself one last time that the truth was best. Taking a deep breath, she met the man's green gaze, full of question. "We were attacked yesterday. Two men came in an'..." She stopped to choose her words carefully for the man of God. "Attempted to force themselves upon us." She swallowed when his mouth dropped open. "Thankfully, Mr. Donegal here was in the area huntin' when he heard our screams an' came to our aid."

Reverend Graham turned to the taller man with wide eyes. "An' what of these men now?" His words were slow and tight, as though he dreaded the answer.

Mr. Donegal's mouth pulled into a frown. "They did not survive, sir." His eyes darted to her, then back. "There was no other way."

Reverend Graham seemed to take a moment to process those words as he turned from the man. "Yes, I can imagine under the circumstances." Still, his words were breathy and his face was pale. Why was he so affected? Death, even brutal ones, was not exactly uncommon in the wilderness. Especially during the Indian raids. "I, um, would like to speak a few words over the graves." He turned back to Mr. Donegal, who gave a quick nod, and it seemed there was a bit more resolve about the minister.

Margaret sagged against the chair back as the men left the cabin together. In all the stress of the night and morning, she had given little thought to the men who had attacked them. Though she was glad they were no longer a threat, her heart ached to think of the lives lost. Quickly surveying the room, Margaret realized that not only had Mr. Donegal buried the bodies, but he must have scrubbed the floors as well. Had she truly slept through all of it?

A creaking of the floorboards drew her attention to the hearth, where Muireall had taken up her embroidery once more. Margaret frowned after the younger girl as a wave of sadness washed over her. What was to become of them?

A few short moments later, Reverend Graham came in alone, stating that Mr. Donegal had gone to tend to his horse. The minister came over and settled on the chair nearest Margaret. He put his hands together, elbows on his knees, as he faced her. "I wish to speak openly with you for a moment."

She nodded.

"Neither you nor your sister were compromised?" He spoke with an earnest concern that softened his sensitive query.

She stiffened as her gaze flicked to her sister and back. How close they had come to just that. But the reverend would not be asking without a good reason, surely. "No."

"And this Donegal fellow has not compromised you?"

"No," she stated with more conviction.

Still, the reverend's mouth pulled down at the corners. "And yet, he has been alone with you two women."

"Only to care for us last night and this morning." She whisked her skirts away to reveal her injury. "I would not want to think where we would be without him." Her voice continued to rise in strength.

Reverend Graham gasped. "Another injury from the struggle?"

"Yes." She almost hissed the word. "My leg was pierced clean through." She should keep her patience with the man, but her blood seemed to heat at the insinuations he was making.

"Well." He stood and quickly averted his gaze. Margaret's hands tightened on her thighs, her gaze pinned on the short man as he paced. "This ordeal only goes to prove that the Kentucky wilderness is no place for a lady to be alone. I will have a word with Mr. Donegal as well, but if he is truly a man of character, I believe it would be best if one of you ladies were to marry the man."

Margaret's head swam as though she had been backhanded again. Despite all Mr. Donegal had done for them over the past day, they had only just met the man. How could they truly know his character? Margaret's stomach roiled. Suddenly, their reverend did not seem quite the man she had thought him to be. Was this who he was when disaster struck? And yet, there was an inkling of truth in his words... for how else would they carry on? She had certainly proved she could not care for her sister alone.

*M*arriage. Iain felt as though his world had been tilted on its axis and switched with that of another person as he stared down at the short, stout reverend. He couldn't marry. The life of a long hunter was not one to be shared with a wife and family. And he could never move back east permanently. Still, the little man prattled on. "I know I do not know you very well." *Nay, ye dinnae.* "But I know of no other man in this area who is of marrying age. And these women cannot continue on their own. Yesterday was proof of that."

Iain swallowed. He could not disagree with Reverend Graham there. His mind went to Margaret, sitting in the cabin with her stitched-up leg and battered face. Something in his chest clenched, and he let out a sigh. He had not walked away before, so what made him think he could walk away and leave her and her sister helpless now? But marriage? There had to be another way. One that did not involve one of the women ruining their life by saddling themselves with his sorry self.

"What if I took them to a fort where they would be safe and could find men of their own choosing to marry?"

The reverend stopped and tilted his head in thought. "That could work. But two women alone with a man in the wilderness? Would people truly believe they were uncompromised when they arrived?"

Iain frowned. It was not unheard of, women using male guides to travel to a new destination after losing their family. But it would put the two in a precarious position.

"Just think on it," Reverend Graham urged.

But Iain's mind was already reeling with the thought of it— the faces of the men and women as he, a grown man, arrived at the fort alone with two beautiful young women. Another sigh rushed out as he turned and pushed a hand through his hair. What had he gotten himself into? Did he really have no other choice if he were to protect the women? A strange sensation rippled through his middle.

He turned and marched into the cabin with the reverend hot on his heels.

He banged open the door, startling Muireall where she sat at the table. "Sorry." Margaret's gaze lifted, a wrinkle across her forehead and her lips pinched. Iain stalked over and sat in the chair in front of her, resisting the urge to take her hands into his. "What do ye want?"

The corners of her mouth turned down, and her gaze darted to Muireall. She took a deep breath before she nodded at her sister. "I want ye to marry Muireall."

Iain sat up straighter, blindsided. He had not considered the younger sister for marriage. Only the one before him who avoided his gaze.

Muireall shot up from the table. "Me? He is old enough to be me father!"

It was doubtful there was an age gap larger than ten years between them. Though perhaps life in the wilderness had aged him beyond his years. Iain certainly felt older than twenty-seven.

"I promised Ma." Margaret's voice was strong as she countered her sister. "The day she died, I promised her I would not let ye die here in the wilderness. I promised to take care of ye, an' I intend to do just that." So saying, she set her jaw.

"An' I have to be married to be taken care of? Ye could still take care of me if ye were the one to marry." The girl's hands went to her hips.

Margaret's bottom lip rolled under as she watched her sister. Though Muireall had a point, the weight of the promises Margaret had made must weigh heavily on her.

Iain sighed and stood. Her gaze followed him, curious. "Look, ye need the full truth before ye make yer decision."

She raised a brow and waited expectantly while her sister glared from across the table.

"I have been around for months, lookin' after ye. When I split wood for meself, I would keep some back an' bring it under the cover of night. I kept an eye on yer food stores, an' when the meat was gone, left the rabbit." He rubbed the back of his neck. Margaret sucked in a breath. He could barely lift his gaze to hers as he continued. "I was movin' through the area when I saw ye buryin' yer mither. I realized ye were alone, with no man to care for ye. So I stayed close, made sure ye stayed afloat."

"We have been starvin' while ye stayed hidden." Muireall spat the words across the table at him, and he cringed. He should have done more.

When Margaret pulled herself up to stand on her good leg, Iain waited for her to throw him out, to spew her outrage at his deception. Instead, she held a hand out to quiet Muireall and kept that curious gaze of hers trained on him. "Why did ye not reveal yerself?"

Iain swallowed. "I never wished to develop ties. I never wished to marry." His jaw clenched, for he was still only giving her a half truth. Her eyes narrowed as though she could tell. How could this woman see through him so easily?

Margaret attempted a step toward him but nearly fell as her face scrunched in pain. He rushed to her, taking her into his arms. Her muscles rigid and her fingers biting into his flesh, she stood tall, meeting his gaze with those eyes filled with a depth of color unlike any he had seen before. Their intensity bore into him.

"If we married, would ye come to resent me?"

"Nay." He breathed the word before considering his answer. The feel of her in his arms arms was so natural, so perfect, that she could never be a regret. He, on the other hand, was another story. Looking at the floor, he stepped back, still supporting her. "Ye might come to resent me, though."

The woman's head tipped to the side as she regarded him. She watched him for a long moment before she turned to Muireall, who still stood with her arms crossed on the other side of the table. Reverend Graham waited quietly by the door, his hands linked behind his back. Margaret's lips pursed before she looked back up into Iain's face. "I suppose that is a risk I must take."

Reverend Graham stepped forward, a smile upon his face. "So we will have a wedding, then?"

Margaret lifted her chin and gave a nod without averting her gaze. Warmth and resolve filled her eyes. Admiration flooded Iain as he stared into her sun-kissed face. If he had ever desired a wife, one with such strength and spirit would have been exactly what he sought. And now, here she stood in his arms, vowing to unite her life with his. *Please dinnae let her come to regret this day, Lord.* He swallowed as doubt swirled in his chest.

CHAPTER 4

Margaret frowned over at her husband as she listened to the slow, even breaths that told her he still slept. Iain's back was turned toward her, the muslin fabric of his shirt pulling across his shoulders. She tapped her fingers along the worn quilt top and attempted to ignore the sensation in her middle that told her she needed to attend to morning matters, and quickly. Muireall slept in her bed across the room, but there was no telling what kind of caterwaulin' they would have to endure if Margaret woke her.

Glancing around the dark cabin, she considered if there were any items in their possession she could use as a walking stick. A wooden-handled broom came to mind, but it was on the far side of the kitchen table, in the corner. A sigh escaped her. Maybe if she held onto the bed and table, she could hobble over? It was worth a shot, considering she might burst otherwise.

Ignoring the pain that shot through her leg where it was stitched together, Margaret pulled the covers aside and dropped her legs over the side of the tick. She carefully eased her weight onto her good leg and then started the tedious journey around the edge of the bed. Having reached the corner post, she attempted to judge the distance to the nearest chair in the darkness. Gathering up her skirts, she took two jumps.

Still, she came up short. Margaret rolled her lips under and eyed her destination. Then, she scrunched down and gave one more one-legged leap. However, this time, when she landed, she faltered and fought for balance. Her torso wavered back and forth as her arms flailed. Grabbing at the chair, she wrapped her fingers around the wooden corner of its back as she fell backward, pulling it with her. Margaret landed unceremoniously on her rear, just before the chair thudded next to her. She cringed and turned to see if anyone had heard.

The rustle of covers told her Iain had. Within a mere moment, even in the pitch black, he was by her side, his shirt askew and his hair disheveled. Concern darkened his gaze. "What happened?" His voice was raspy as he reached for her, placing a hand on her arm as he glanced her and the situation over.

"I was tryin' to make me way over to the broom to use as a walkin' stick. I, uh, need to tend to matters." Was the heat that spread over her cheeks from embarrassment or the nearness of her new husband? His hand was warm and reassuring at her elbow, his face barely a foot away from hers.

"Oh." He glanced away, and his throat bobbed as he swallowed. "Would ye rather have me or yer sister help ye outside?"

Margaret grimaced toward her slumbering sister. Iain seemed to read her mind.

"Come on." He moved closer to ease an arm around her shoulders.

Once they were standing, he gave her a moment to adjust and lean on him before they began the trek outdoors. She forgot her embarrassment for a moment as she melted into the comfort of his presence. Maybe today would be different from the one prior.

As soon as their wedding had concluded and Reverend Graham had departed, Iain had dismissed himself to hunt. While he had brought down a large buck, whose meat would see them through for some time, he had not returned until just before dark. Then, though he agreed to share her parents' bed with her, he had slept with his back toward her. It was certainly not the wedding, or wedding night, she had imagined for herself. Though their union was one born of necessity, as they spoke their vows, she had imagined passing the afternoon learning more of the man she would be spending her life with. Instead, loneliness and disappointment had been her companions.

But now, with his arm wrapped around her, hope stirred that their situation might turn for the better. After all, his eyes had reflected genuine concern as he had knelt before her. And as they hobbled out into the cool morning air, it seemed that their bodies had been cut from the same cloth, fitting with one another like a missing piece.

~

"Iain!" He whirled at Margaret calling his name two days later. His heart kicked up a notch, though nothing in her voice implied distress. Abandoning the deerskin he had strung up to begin the tanning process, he hastened around the barn, toward the house.

Margaret stood in the doorway of the cabin, hands on her hips. Shaking his head, he continued forward, fighting the smile that threatened to bloom on his face. How was it, when he had been determined not to form ties, that he had come to be married to the most spirited and captivating woman he had ever laid eyes on? Still, he could not allow her to fall in love with him. He could not risk her heart in that way.

Stepping onto the porch, Iain opened his mouth to ask

Margaret how she had made it outside, but she did not give him a chance before she spoke.

"Food is on the table." She lifted her chin and met him square in the eye.

Iain raised his brows. "How?"

"I found an old crutch me pa used the year he broke his leg." Margaret's gaze did not waver, nor the tilt of her chin, but a muscle in her jaw worked. Likely, she was finding it difficult to maintain her stance as she kept her back straight and only a hand on the doorframe.

Iain narrowed his gaze. "Where?"

This time, his wife swallowed. Her gaze darted to the barn and back. Iain wanted to let out a groan, but he waited for her to answer. "In the barn." He started to protest, but she continued. "I used the broom to get there."

"Margaret." Iain did not mean to, but her name came out as a growl as he stepped closer. Her eyes widened as she looked up at him, and he let out a sigh. He brought a hand up to her arm, keeping his touch at her wrist where the sleeve of her dress still separated their skin. "Ye have to be careful 'n' rest, or ye will never heal." He kept his voice as tender as he could as he appealed to her.

The stubborn little lass simply crossed her arms and leaned against the doorway. "An' there are still chores that need to be tended to an' meals that need prepared."

Iain found himself inching closer as his ire rose. "An' yer sister can handle those tasks."

Margaret gave him a look that told him he knew better than to expect such of Muireall. His gaze darted from her face to the interior of the cabin. He could only guess where the girl was—embroidering in the chair by the hearth. How had the child become so spoiled? Iain had half a mind to stalk in there and demand that she assist her sister...again. But he did not wish to form a riff between family.

"Fine. Come in an' we will eat," he offered instead.

Margaret nodded before she turned and pulled her crude crutch from where it was hidden, leaned against the inside wall. Iain gaped as she awkwardly inserted the crutch, which was easily a foot too tall for her, under her arm and hobbled forward. He followed with a shake of his head, the smell of burnt venison hitting him as he followed her to the table.

"I will cut that down to fit ye better after we eat." If his wife insisted upon working, it was the least he could do. "But ye really should be restin'."

Margaret turned to him. "An' as I told ye, there is too much to be done to be lyin' in bed all day."

"Ye should have help." Iain's voice rose as he threw a glare in Muireall's direction. The girl sat exactly where he had thought her to be.

Margaret ignored him and instead called to her sister. "Time to eat."

"Just a moment." Muireall's voice belied her exasperation, as though the meal were an inconvenience rather than a blessing.

Iain's muscles tensed, but he kept his attention on Margaret, who stood waiting for him to take a seat. Instead, he moved over and pulled out the chair beside her. "Sit," he ordered with more force than he had intended as he nodded toward the seat.

Margaret dropped into it, cringing at the pain that must have reverberated through her leg. She seemed to deflate, her shoulders sagging as she relaxed into the chair. It was as though a great burden had been lifted from her, and the action sent a tugging sensation through Iain's chest. He turned and eyed her indolent sister.

"Muireall," he barked. "Yer sister has done worked herself to the bone to put a meal on the table for ye. Leave yer sewin' an' come show her some respect. An' after supper, I expect ye to clear the dishes an' wash 'em. Yer sister needs to rest."

Muireall pinned him with a glare before she dropped her sewing in a basket and strode over to the table, plopping down in her seat with her arms crossed like an impish child's. As he settled into his own chair, the heat of his wife's gaze burned into the side of his face. But a glance in her direction showed admiration, not anger, reflected in her gaze. She bowed her head to offer grace.

"Thank Ye, Lord, for Yer blessin's upon us," her melodic voice began softly. "Thank Ye for the family members around this table. An' for our health. An' thank Ye for the bounty of this food, Lord. Amen."

Iain lifted his head as she closed the prayer and dug in. Ignoring the charring on the meat, he was determined to fill his belly and return to the deer hide.

"So, Iain," Margaret began beside him. He froze. "I need to know if ye can keep Muireall safe here. Or if ye believe it would be best to take her back east or somewhere else safer."

"What?" Muireall's fork clattered onto her tin plate, and her eyes widened. "I thought all was settled. Yer married now. He can keep us safe." Tears swam in the girl's deep-blue eyes, and for the first time since he had met her, Iain felt a stirring of compassion for her. After the loss of her parents, fear must have driven itself deep within her bones.

Iain looked from her to Margaret, whose mouth was pressed thinner than his. She needed him to address this situation as well.

"Nowhere is truly safe. Not in these times. There is a war among the peoples as to who should settle this land. An' the results are not pretty. Not only are there Chickamauga Cherokee who have branched off from their nation to fight for this land, but the British enlisted the help of the Shawnee to besiege Kentucky settlements. One man cannae stand against an army. Trust me." Instead of glancing at Muireall, who was the one who needed convincing, he looked to his wife. To the compassion that shone in those enchanting eyes as her gaze roamed the side of his face, to the place where any other man would have an ear. Instead, he boasted only the battle scars proving how dangerous their situation was. And how inadequate he was to protect them.

"Then where should we go?" Margaret's voice was infused with confidence—in him.

And suddenly, he felt unworthy to make the decision. A greater man would likely whisk them back east of the mountains. But he was incapable of doing so, incapable of doing the one thing that might truly ensure their safety. He could not risk the temptation that was so abundant there. The temptation that would make him a liability to these woman rather than a help. Instead, he would stand by what he had discussed with the reverend and take them to a fort. Somewhere where there were more men and guns to protect them should an attack occur. A cross-country trip would keep him from growing roots and keep his wife focused on the journey rather than their relationship, anyway.

"I will escort ye to Fort Harrod. It is the closest outpost, an' we can likely make the journey within a week. Though, we will need to wait until yer healed enough." Iain gave his wife a pointed look.

Her mouth twisted, but she nodded her assent. Muireall gaped at them, but Margaret paid her no attention. "An' we will live there?"

"Aye. In or near the fort. It is a civilian fort built by those that settled Harrodstown for the sole purpose of providin' protection from Indian attacks. An' now from the British as well. Most people stay for a while until they move on to another location or build a home nearby where they can still come into the fort if there is threat of attack."

Margaret regarded him thoughtfully. "Good," she agreed before turning back to her food.

As Iain attempted to return to his own meal, the sound of forks scraping on tin grated on his nerves, setting him on edge. Though they were sitting ducks in the cabin, they would not be much better on the trail. One could never know where they would encounter trouble. And life had shown him incapable of protecting those in his care once before. He would always bear the scars proving so. Suddenly, responsibility settled heavily over his shoulders. Would he actually be able to deliver these two women to safety?

⁓

"*A*n' keep the door barred." Iain's pale-blue eyes were intense as he leveled a look at her through the half-open door.

"Aye," Margaret agreed, keeping most of the exasperation from her voice.

Iain's gaze dropped from her eyes to her lips, and for the briefest of moments, she thought he might lean in and bridge the gap between them. Her heart beat in anticipation as she leaned toward him. But in a flash, he was gone without another word. Just as every day of the week and a half since their marriage. Margaret's shoulders sagged, and she let out a sigh as she closed the door, barring it behind her. *Lord, please keep him safe an' guide his path.*

Though her husband had seemed intent on avoiding her at all costs, having come up with daily excuses as to what needed tending before their travel, she had come to enjoy the comfort of his presence. And while it was frustrating, his reasons for being apart were always valid. There truly was a great deal that had to be done to ensure they had a successful journey. A journey which would finally begin of a morrow.

Anticipation thrummed through Margaret as she turned and glanced about the cabin. Though their belongings were meager, most everything had already been packed away. Still, she itched for some tasks to busy her idle hands and occupy her time. It would be some time before her husband returned from scouting out the best place for them to cross the Green River, and she did not intend to sit about the cabin like some forlorn puppy.

Though the efforts would soon be wasted, Margaret set about dusting and washing every surface available to her—the shelf, the table, the chairs. And when those had been completed, she moved on to the floor. Her leg, with the stitches having been removed two nights before, still ached. But her pain had subsided to a dull sensation she could easily ignore as she accomplished her tasks.

Halfway through sweeping, Margaret stopped to wipe sweat and grime from her forehead. "Can ye move yer chair, please?"

Muireall's gaze was hostile as she dragged it from the embroidery she had refused to pack. "Why are ye even botherin' with cleanin' this place when we will be leavin' it behind directly?"

Margaret placed a hand on her hip as she leaned on the broom. "An' what does it hurt? Pa built this house with his own two hands. We might be leavin', but I intend to leave it in the best condition I can." She glanced pointedly at the embroidery her sister had spent hours working since their mother passed, then took a swipe with her broom beneath the chair her sister had never moved. "An' some of us need somethin' to occupy our time." She went on sweeping toward the bed.

"I still dinnae understand why we have to leave at all. Ye took that man as a husband. He is supposed to protect us."

The whine in her sister's voice grated on Margaret's nerves, as did her words. Margaret whirled toward Muireall, her eyes filled with tears. "Like Pa protected us?" The color drained from her sister's face. "Life happens, Muireall. People get sick and hurt, even men. It is just as Iain said, there is nowhere truly safe. He knows that all too well."

"His ear." Muireall sneered, as though she had read her mind. "Ye dinnae know how he lost it. Ye dinnae know the man at all. He could be playin' us both!"

Margaret jerked back as though she had been slapped. How dare Muireall? Defensiveness surged in red-hot anger, boiling up the back of her neck and into her cheeks. "The man kept us afloat when we were nothin' to him. An' he has done nothin' but care for us since we were married. Where do ye think we would be right now if he had not shown himself when he did?" The thought caused her stomach to roil.

Muireall only faltered for a moment. "An' where would we be had Reverend Graham not arrived an' all but forced marriage on the two of ye? Would Iain still be around?" She lifted her dark brows, and her gaze bore into Margaret. "He sure does not seem to want to be married to ye. He disappears at every turn, an' I have not seen him touch ye once! Not even a tiny peck on the cheek."

Margaret had stayed strong for her sister so many times, but now she stood with tears in her eyes, her own sister the one to tear her down. Grating her teeth against one another, she lifted her chin. "Just because we have not been married long does not mean he will not come to love me. He has been busy preparin' for our journey an' providin' food for our table. I would rather have that than kisses any day." Even as the words left her lips, Margaret knew they were only half true. Still, she turned on her heel and marched to the door, lifting the bar.

"What are ye doin? Where are ye goin'?"

Margaret ignored the protests that trailed behind her and marched, as best she could, across the porch and out to the barn. Entering the dark, musty building, she wiped at the tears that slid down her cheeks, her heart aching more than it had in months. A nicker nearly startled her out of her skin, but then a smile spread across her face as Iain's palomino mare poked her head over her stall door.

"Hey, girl," Margaret whispered as she approached, rubbing a hand over the soft skin of the horse's nose, then up into her buttery-colored coat. The mare nuzzled her neck, easing the ache in her heart and quelling the scared, tender voice inside her that questioned whether her husband would ever come to love her. For even though she barely knew him, she longed for him to.

There was no doubt, she was not beautiful. Her hair shared the same color as the dirt below her feet, while her eyes could not even choose a single color. Blue, green, and gold all mixed together within their depths. Plain, drab, and unremarkable—that was her. Her own mother had preferred her sister, showering Muireall with attention and praise while Margaret was left to tend to the chores. If her own blood had not loved her, how could she expect a man who been pressed into marrying her to? A sob erupted from her throat as a fresh wave of tears sprang forth.

CHAPTER 5

Iain hurried down the hillside to the cabin while crickets chirped all around. Lightning bugs danced in the dark, reminding him how long he had been absent from his wife. A chill unrelated to the night rippled through him, but he simply moved faster over the ground he had come to know quite well. As he leapt onto the porch, his boots thudded on the wood, then echoed with each step as he strode forward. When he pushed against the door and found it still barred, a breath whooshed from his lungs. He knocked quickly and heartily. "Margaret, it is me, darlin'." His neck heated at the unintentional endearment that slipped from his tongue. But he needed the women to know there was nothing to fear.

When the wooden barrier swung open, though, his heart dropped to the floor. "Where's Margaret?" He pushed past Muireall and into the cabin, where his gaze quickly swept over the room. His wife nowhere in sight, he looked back to her sister, whose wide eyes were red and puffy.

"I dinnae know. We had an argument, an' she left," the girl cried.

Suddenly, Iain struggled for air. "Ye let her leave? An' ye

have no idea where she went to?" His voice came out in a boom that made the girl flinch.

She shook her head frantically.

Iain's gaze swept to the inky night outside the still-open door, the black of which reflected the hopelessness that swirled within him. *Dear God, let me find her.* Iain sent the desperate plea up as he stalked past Muireall and out of the house. He strode across the porch, then jogged the short distance across the clearing and threw the barn door open, only to be greeted with an even darker void. The only thing he could make out in the bleak interior was Goldie's light head. She let out a nicker at the sight of him, but he had no time for the animal.

"Margaret," he bellowed.

A stirring noise made his heart leap, but it came from the direction of the horse's stall. When the horse lowered her head, his shoulders sagged.

He faced the door. "Margaret!" If she had ventured off into the countryside, how would he ever find her at night?

~

*M*argaret bolted upright at the sound of her name being yelled. Brushing hay from her hair, she shot to her feet. Had it truly been her husband's voice that echoed through the barn, laced with a haunting desperation? Aye, there he stood, a dark figure silhouetted by the dim moonlight that eased into the building through a break in the clouds. "Iain?"

In answer, the tall, slender man rushed forward. Without a word, he entered the stall and took her into his arms. One strong hand slipped around her waist, drawing her closer, while the other went to the side of her face. His callused fingers brushed over her cheek, causing warmth to ripple through her middle, before they entwined in her hair. Margaret's lips parted as Iain's forehead settled against hers. Instinctively, her arms wrapped around his waist as she leaned into the intimate embrace.

"What happened?" The words rumbled out of his chest.

"Me an' Muireall argued. I needed to get away for a bit, but I must have fallen asleep talkin' to Goldie." Her own voice was breathless as she spoke. Iain pulled her even closer, drawing her head in to nestle on his shoulder. Cradled in his warm hug, Margaret could almost imagine that he loved her, that God had made them perfect for one another. But Muireall's words came flooding back to her. As she pulled back, her brows bunched together. "Did ye only just come home?"

Iain's face fell as he sighed, avoiding her gaze. "It took me longer than expected to scout out the best route."

Margaret nodded, her lips pressed together. Had he meant to stay away all the day? Either way, she had wifely duties to attend to. It was well past time for them all to have eaten. She withdrew from his embrace. "I suppose yer hungry."

Exiting the stall, she lifted her chin and headed toward the cabin, leaving her husband behind. A moment later, his footfalls followed behind her.

Catching her hand, he stopped her in her tracks. "What did ye an' Muireall argue about?"

Margaret's mouth dropped open before she looked to the ground. She needed to find some way to explain without divulging her insecurities. "She still does not understand why we are leavin'." Did he believe her? She chanced a glance in his direction.

"She is young. An' that was all?" He drew her closer, sliding a hand about her waist.

Margaret's lips parted as she stared up at him, the pale moonlight catching in the blue of his eyes. All the breath left her body. "She does not trust ye yet."

Iain's brows pulled together, as did his lips, and her insides began to squirm. "What did she say?"

"'Twas nothin'. She will come around."

One brow lifted. "'Tisn't nothin', or I wouldn't a found ye in the barn."

Margaret swallowed. How could her husband see through her so easily? Her husband...the man who had little choice but marry her, yet now held her as though he found her desirable. What was the truth? She looked down again, not able to bear the gleam in his eyes. "She said ye might not be bein' honest with us. An' that ye wouldn't be around if it wasn't for Reverend Graham all but forcin' marriage on ye."

Margaret could feel the breath leave Iain's body, the sag of his muscles at the impact of her words. A hand came under her chin and tipped it upward so that her eyes met his again. "Not a word I have told ye has not been the truth." His gaze was intense on hers for a moment as his words settled in.

Then he brought his mouth down to hers. At the sweet caress of his lips, she pushed onto her toes to better meet him. His arm wrapped tighter about her waist as his other hand moved into her hair, drawing her closer with a tender passion. For the first time in her life, Margaret felt...wanted. Leaning into her husband's warm embrace, she pressed into the feeling.

But all too soon, Iain pulled away, keeping only his forehead touching hers. "I could go for that dinner now," he whispered huskily.

Margaret could only nod, her thoughts far from food. Could her husband care more for her than he had been letting on? Hope blossomed in her chest and spread outward to warm her cheeks.

A smile stretched across Margaret's face as she marched through the sun-strewn forest with her husband ahead of her and his beautiful palomino alongside her on the hillside. Sunlight slanted through breaks in the treetops overhead, casting beams of light over the ferns and moss at their bases. Majestic cardinals flitted among the branches, while bushy-tailed squirrels chattered at their approach. Iain ducked under a low-hanging grapevine and looked back to make sure she did the same.

Her gaze darted down to the grassy carpet below them, recollections of the night before fresh in her mind. Though he had appeared all business when they awoke this morning, she could not erase the memory of their kiss. Combined with the endless possibilities that stretched before them as they began their journey, Margaret could not help the elation that had surged through her as she had stepped out into the warm sunlight.

Not even her sister's moping could dampen Margaret's mood. Though Muireall had seemed to have calmed since their argument the day before, she was as downtrodden as ever, walking about like a meek field mouse with not a friend in the world. She had offered no apology, though, and the two had discussed matters no further.

Margaret, on the other hand, could rest assured that her husband must find her at least somewhat attractive. And just as significant as the kiss, she could not forget the concern that had shown on his face both when he found her and afterward, as he pressed her to share her burdens with him.

Distracted, she nearly ran into the subject of her thoughts as he stopped and turned toward her, rifle in hand. An ounce of that same concern and intensity shone in his gaze now. "This is where we start our descent. The way will be steep an' difficult. If the mare falls and starts sliding, let her go."

Margaret nodded before glancing toward the horse, then over the animal's neck to her sister. Muireall's eyes had become like large saucers as she hugged her arms around herself. But without a word, they continued on.

As Iain had warned, the almost-imperceptible trail they followed steepened as the earth tipped toward the river waiting at the bottom of the rise. To avoid a tree that had fallen over the path, he guided them into a rain-washed rut which was littered with little tan rocks. Margaret ran her hands farther down toward the end of the reins, to allow the horse more room to move and keep her balance as the animal picked her way across the higher ground to her right. Muireall moved in behind her, grunting and groaning at the uneven terrain. Margaret rolled her eyes but kept close attention on her own steps as she followed Iain down to where the gulley opened up into a wider trail. Muddied and speckled with animal prints, it brought them to where the hillside gave way to the river.

Margaret grinned as she stepped onto the rock-strewn shore.

Golden rays of sunshine filtered through the trees above them, causing the ripples in the blue-green water to sparkle. A great blue heron stood in the shadows beyond the sandbar that cut through the middle of the river, while an endless expanse of green stretched up the hillside beyond. Peace abounded as only the quiet gurgle of the water met their ears. Sighing, Margaret turned in a circle as she gazed up at a spectacularly blue sky spotted only by a sparse amount of fluffy white clouds. The warmth of the sun kissed her skin.

Finally, Iain's clearing of his throat broke her reverie. She turned toward him with wide eyes, for she must have looked like a little child. But an odd grin quirked one side of his mouth while he seemed to fight to hide it. "We will cross here." With an attempt to keep his voice serious, he nodded toward the sandbar in the middle of the majestic Green River.

"What?" Muireall's eyes rounded as she looked at them over the horse's withers.

"Aye. A river crossin'." Margaret faced her. "Do ye not remember our journey west?"

Less than five years had passed since the Blair family had traveled from Virginia to Kentucky, a journey which had contained many more daunting crossings than the one they were about to embark upon.

"Aye," her sister agreed in a quiet voice as she turned to eye the river as though it might come up and eat them.

Though their father's death had been a freak accident caused by nature, a frozen branch having broken loose and fallen atop him, Margaret still did not understand the fear that had taken root in her sister since. Perhaps her own faith was stronger than Muireall's? Should she have been a better sister, sharing her faith more? Her mouth twisted.

"Ye both know how to swim?" Iain lifted his dark brows, drawing her attention back to him.

Margaret nodded.

"Good. The crossin' is shallow enough ye should not have to, but 'tis still good to be prepared. I will lead the way. Follow in me footsteps as best ye can." He moved toward Margaret and took Goldie's reins from her. "I will take her across with me so yer not encumbered." He caught her gaze, and the concern etched across his forehead caused a ripple of fear to course through her.

Margaret nodded. She would go last to ensure Muireall made it across safely. She had to fulfill her promise to keep her sister safe.

Iain sloshed into the water, taking confident steps as Goldie fearlessly and obediently strode alongside him. Margaret turned to Muireall, but the girl still remained frozen as she stared at the blue-green depths. "Come on, Muireall." She moved closer and nudged her forward. "Remember the swimming hole? Stay close to Iain, an' ye will be safe."

Her sister frowned, but she took the first tentative step into the water. Margaret came behind, the cool water rising around her ankles, then working its way up to her waist. The day's warmth made it bearable. Muireall gasped several times as they moved deeper, but the water never rose over their chests, and their feet never left the ground before they began to climb onto the sandbar in the middle where Iain waited with Goldie. Thankfully, the dune was dense and rocky rather than truly sandy, so Margaret walked across without fear that one of them or the heavily packed mare might sink.

Iain stepped into the second stretch of water, but once again, Muireall hesitated. Her eyes darted back and forth as though some menace might leap from the water at any moment. Meanwhile, the great blue heron still stood unperturbed a short distance down the river. When she finally stepped forward, Margaret followed, only to have her sister scramble backward and knock her over.

"Snake," Muireall shrieked as she pointed upstream.

Righting herself, Margaret dusted her hands off and peered at the long black form gliding toward them. Indeed, water snakes could pose a danger in the area. But she shook her head and made a slight scoffing sound. "Muireall. It is a stick. See?" She pointed as the harmless piece of wood slipped by on the current.

With the help of a slight push, her sister resumed her course, with Margaret behind. This time, as they neared the deepest part, the water came nearly to Margaret's shoulders. Taking a deep breath, she continued on—until Muireall screamed and lashed out. As the water swirled around Margaret's neck, Muireall's arm crashed down on her head. It knocked her feet out from under her, and she fell backward, under the water. She resurfaced after only a moment.

Muireall thrashed about as though she could not swim.

"Muireall. Muireall. Calm down." Margaret swam toward her. She reached for her sister, but the girl continued to gasp and slash at the water, making it difficult to reach her. Finally, Margaret dipped under the water and grabbed her around the waist. This only made her struggle worse.

Her sister bucked and kicked, catching her foot in Margaret's petticoats. Margaret was jerked into the depths. Disoriented in the murky, churning water, she reached for her petticoats. Searching and tugging, she attempted to dislodge herself from her sister. To no avail.

Even under the water, she could hear her sister yelling. Which was rivaled only by her own lungs screaming for air. Just when she thought she could hold her breath no longer, Muireall was pulled through the water, her foot slipping free from Margaret's dress.

Surging to the surface, Margaret gasped for air. Iain was hauling her sister onto the shore, kicking and screaming. She took a few ragged breaths as she treaded water before following them. But the moment after Iain deposited Muireall on solid ground, he turned back for Margaret, wide-eyed. As soon as she started to wade ashore, he grabbed her hand and helped her.

He pulled her close as his eyes searched hers. "Are ye all right?"

Margaret nodded, her breathing still labored as she recovered from the ordeal. Or could it be from the bright blue eyes that bore into hers with a heat that made her forget that she was drenched head to toe, her petticoats so full of water that they tugged at her waist?

CHAPTER 6

"I am well." Margaret nodded and water dripped from her nose. Though she must look like a half-drowned rat, she was safe. And with her hands gripping her husband's forearms as he held her waist, she was not cold. Her heart pounded in her chest, echoing in her ears.

Iain reached up and pushed aside a strand of hair that was plastered to her forehead, his touch feather-soft against her skin. Margaret closed her eyes. If only they could stay in that moment forever. But all too soon, her husband moved away.

Letting out a small sigh, she leaned forward and wrung as much water as she could from her skirts. Then she moved over to where Muireall huddled on the ground. Kneeling before her, she placed a hand on her sister's drenched sleeve. "Are ye well?"

Round, dark eyes stared up at her from a face that was even paler that usual. Tears seeped down her cheeks as she began to rock. "I cannae do this."

Margaret's heart ached for her sister, who suddenly seemed so much younger than seventeen. "Aye, ye can. 'Tis only a week's journey. Then ye will be somewhere safe. For good."

A shadow fell over them as Iain came to stand near Margaret's shoulder. "An' if we keep movin', we will make Pitman's Station before nightfall."

Muireall glanced at him then, a tiny glimmer of hope in her eyes. "We will?"

Iain nodded.

"See?" Margaret wrung out her sister's skirts as well, then held her hand out. "Come along, an' ye can have a warm, safe place to lay yer head tonight."

Still shaking, Muireall placed a cold hand in hers and stood. Wrapping an arm around her sister's shoulders, Margaret followed Iain as he picked a trail through the undergrowth, heading up the steep hillside. If she could only get her sister safely to Pitman's Station, the first leg of their journey would be complete. And they would be one step closer to Fort Harrod and safety.

~

Merely standing outside William Pitman's large, fortified cabin, unease gnawed at Iain's midsection. The cabin itself was looming, with its second level larger than the first to allow room for gun ports, but several other cabins could be spotted within walking distance. In total, Pitman had explained, there were somewhere around twenty cabins in their little settlement. Iain swallowed and attempted to shift upwind of the smoke from Pitman's pipe.

How could he ever live at Fort Harrod when even the size of this encampment made him feel as though his skin was crawling?

Iain glanced toward his wife, who stood talking with Muireall and Sallie Pitman. The women had both changed their clothing since their arrival and seemed in much better spirits. Margaret's cheeks held a rosy glow as she watched attentively to how the middle-aged woman prepared her stew over the big outdoor firepit. Her long brown hair had been brushed and laid invitingly over the shoulder of a mulberry-colored bodice that made her simply radiant. His heart ached and his insides twisted to think that he might disappoint her. And sooner rather than later.

"Where are you headed, again?" Pitman's brusque voice pulled him back to the conversation at hand.

"Fort Harrod," Iain replied tightly, not taking his eyes off his wife.

"Ah, not too far a journey. And how far have you already traveled?"

Iain glanced at the man who appeared middle-aged, much like Mrs. Pitman, though his hair remained darker, while hers already held a smattering of gray. "Only a day's journey."

Pitman gave a *humph* before he took another draw on the pipe and motioned toward the women. "And the older sister is your wife?"

"Aye."

"Hmm." Pitman nodded. "The younger one sure is a beauty."

"Aye." Though he had no designs on the woman, Iain could acknowledge that she would be beautiful to most men. But her attitude certainly diminished that fairness once a person knew the lass better, and Margaret was the one that captivated him inside and out. She stirred within him emotions that had long been stuffed in the bureau of his heart and locked with a key. Somehow, though, she was breaking her way inside.

"No children yet?"

The man's question froze Iain in his spot. Children? He swallowed, wishing more than ever for a good excuse to depart from the man's company. But the horse had already been fed and watered and their belongings packed inside. "Nay," he finally responded. "We have not been married long." He added the last part in hopes that it would delay further questioning on the matter.

"Ah, just trust in God's timing. We waited plenty of years before He blessed us with our John." Pitman nodded toward where a lanky six-year-old threw rocks over the bluff into Sinking Creek to their right with a couple of other boys. The next minute, one said something to the other, and the trio took off running past them.

Something within Iain's chest tightened. He could never have that, never be a father. He had proven to himself long ago that he would never be suited. And he could not do that to any child. His gaze drew back to Margaret in her mulberry bodice. Or to her.

~

"How much farther?"

Margaret frowned as her sister's whining voice came drifting up from somewhere behind her. She glanced toward where the sun was beginning to settle over the treetops, casting a beautiful golden hue over the earth. "Soon," she told Muireall, a smile in her voice.

Though her legs ached and her feet were likely covered up with blisters, it was an enchanting countryside they hiked through, following the path of the creek that surrounded three sides of Pitman's Station before heading north. The water provided a glorious babble as birds chirped and green abounded in every direction. Kentucky was truly a fertile wilderness, waiting to be explored. If only it could be done in peace. As quiet as their journey had been since they departed from the Pitmans' earlier that morning, it was easy to forget why they were on the journey to begin with—that there was a brutal and bloody war partly over whether they should be there at all. Margaret's smile dipped into a frown.

Suddenly, Iain stopped and motioned for them to do the same. Margaret halted in her tracks, and Muireall drew up close behind her. Without a word, Iain handed Goldie's reins to Margaret. Then, sweeping his gaze across the countryside, he crept across the creek and through the trees.

Margaret's pulse picked up as she watched and waited, the silence weighing heavily on her. Had he noticed some danger and gone to assess the situation? The minutes seemed to tick by with aching slowness as she held the leather reins tight in her grip.

Goldie stomped and snorted, startling her nearly out of her skin.

"Sorry, girl," she whispered as she rubbed the mount's cream-colored neck without taking her gaze from the gap between trees where her husband had disappeared.

Finally, Iain re-emerged, seemingly intact and unharmed. Still, she fidgeted with the reins while she waited for him to approach. Unfortunately, the stubborn man offered no explanation, and his face held no answers. "This way," was all he said as he took the reins from her and led Goldie back the way he had come.

Margaret pursed her lips but trailed after him. After sloshing through the cold, shallow creek, they wound their way among a stand of pines before coming to an opening in the rock. Margaret stopped, her mouth dropping open as Iain walked in, horse and all.

After a second's hesitation, she followed, her short-heeled boots clicking on the sandstone floor much the same as Goldie's hooves. Though the cave initially appeared pitch-black, as she entered, light from the outside trickled in enough for a person to keep their bearings. The room was smaller than a cabin, but it allowed their entire party to move unhindered while a spring filtered down the right side of the cave, out into the creek beyond.

Immediately, Iain started unloading their packs from the mare's back, relieving her of her burden. Margaret set to helping. Once the task was complete, Iain turned to her. "Can ye water the mare in the spring while I gather wood?"

Margaret nodded and took the reins from him. Once Iain had exited, she led the mare over to the little spring and bent to cup some water for herself. But Muireall's voice stopped her in her tracks. "We are staying *here*?" The disgust in her tone was evident.

Margaret whirled on her sister. "Aye. At least ye have a roof over yer head. An' the cave is relatively hidden rather than us lyin' out in the open where we are sittin' ducks for any danger that might come."

Muireall's eyes widened, and she took a step back as though she had been slapped, the color draining from her face.

Margaret sighed. "I am sorry, Muireall, but it is the truth. Ye know we will be sleepin' on the ground an' anywhere else Iain deems is the safest over the next few days. I know ye might not hold him in the highest regard, but ye have to admit, he has more experience than we do. Yer goin' to have to trust him. An' the Lord." She stepped forward and placed a hand on her sister's arm. "Why dinnae ya pull out Ma's Bible an' read a bit of it while I gather firewood?"

Muireall glanced tentatively at the packs, which had been leaned against the wall to Margaret's left, then gave a nod.

"Good." Margaret gave her sister's arm a gentle squeeze before she let go. "Maybe ye will find some comfort there." She offered Muireall a small smile, then knelt once again for a drink of water.

The words of the Bible had always offered her comfort, no matter what their family was going through, and she prayed it could do the same for Muireall. Though above all else, a talk with God was what could truly bring peace to her soul. *Lord, please help Muireall take comfort in Yer Word. But more than anythin', please help her draw near to Ye. Please help her seek Ye an' draw her comfort from Ye.*

~

*I*ain fought to keep his eyes open as he concentrated on pulling the needle through the supple deerskin. Blinking, he allowed a yawn to escape as he attempted to put the last few stitches in a set of moccasins for Margaret. The embers beside him were dying, and barely enough light remained for him to see his work, but he was determined to finish before morning.

Iain's gaze ventured from the leather in his hands to Margaret's bare feet peeking out from under her petticoats. Though she would still be in pain for several days while her blisters and sores healed, he could not bear the thought of allowing her to stuff her feet back into the shoes that had wreaked such havoc on them. Thankfully, she had brought a salve along that would soothe and aid the healing. Iain had insisted that she let him to be the one to smooth it over her injuries so that not a spot was missed.

Ow! He had stuck his finger while regarding his wife's dainty feet. Focusing, he tied off the last stitch and returned his needle and supplies to their pack. Then he gathered the moccasins and moved to where Margaret rested peacefully atop the sole bearskin in his possession. Though the smell had caused a cute wrinkle in her nose, she had expressed her gratitude for the thick fur and settled onto it without hesitation.

Iain stopped to admire her features one more time before he doused the fire with a small tin of water. Warmth and admiration stirred within him as he watched the slow rise and fall of his wife's chest. The longer he knew the woman, the more she proved her mettle...and the more his affection for her grew, much to his chagrin. But try as he might to keep his distance, Margaret was surely a woman to be praised. After two days on the trail, she had not complained once. And though tiredness and pain were their companions, she had not let on to either. Both her grit and determination were admirable.

After ensuring the embers had all died, Iain settled the moccasins on the cave floor beside his wife, then moved in behind her for whatever was left of the night. As he bent to remove his boots, his elbow grazed her back.

Margaret gasped and bolted upright. "Wh-what?" Her hand went to his arm as she glanced about.

Margaret's eyes were so large and innocent that the sight stole the breath from his lungs. Her touch was so light, yet it still bore right through his shirtsleeve to his skin. "Shh. It was only me," he whispered, reaching up to brush a lock of brown hair from her face.

Margaret released a relieved sigh and nodded, but her grip on his arm tightened as her gaze came up to his. Iain's blood coursed faster. Until his wife's brows pulled together. "Are ye just now lyin' down?"

"Aye. Ye have a pair of moccasins for the mornin'." He nodded to where they lay even though they could not be seen in the darkness.

Margaret glanced in their direction, then turned back to him. Her face shone with happiness and gratitude as she tilted her head toward him affectionately. "Oh, Iain." She moved closer to him, bringing a hand up to the side of his face. He closed his eyes at her tender touch and his name on her lips. It was nearly enough to do a man in, to be appreciated so. "Ye didna have to do that."

He raised a brow. "Aye, I did. I could not let ye continue in those shoes."

Margaret returned his pointed look with one of her own,

but a smile tugged at her beautiful lips. It was enough to set his own mouth to turning upward, against his will. This time, he was the one to bring a hand to her face. He rubbed his thumb over her cheek as she leaned into his touch. "Ye should not have to suffer," he whispered, a tugging sensation in his chest.

The simple look of tender appreciation that his wife gave him made him lose his breath. Her glance dropped to his lips, and it was as though he could read her thoughts, hear her asking if it was acceptable for her to kiss him. To express her thanks in a way only a wife could.

For a moment, Iain warred with himself. To give in was to encourage the love between them, to set Margaret up for heartbreak down the road. But then again, he could not bring himself to break her heart at the moment, either, to cause pain by rejecting her affections. So, instead of doing what was sensible, he captured his wife's lips with his. Hers parted, presumably in surprise, as he looped an arm behind her back and pulled her to him. But then her arms came up around his neck, and she leaned into him, answering and exploring as though it was exactly what they were meant to do.

Iain pushed a hand into her hair and cradled the back of her head as he deepened their kiss, allowing their bodies to mold as one. How could something so wonderful ever end in heartbreak? The thought wormed its way into his consciousness and gave him both hope and hesitation. Could the passion that coursed between him and his wife be stronger than what had brought his parents together? For his father, there had been no love in his heart once children came along. So had it been love or simply lustful attraction? And which was this? How was he to know how deeply his feelings for his own wife ran?

Iain forced himself to pull back and take a breath. He kept his eyes closed and his forehead pressed against Margaret's, though. If this was an illusion, he could not bring himself to shatter it. Not yet. So instead, he pressed a kiss to her forehead, then pulled her into his arms as he settled onto the fur. As she nestled into his embrace, he hoped exhaustion would claim him quickly so he did not have to ponder their situation any further. For the feel of his wife in his arms was heavenly.

CHAPTER 7

Margaret knelt at the edge of the crystal-clear creek to splash the cool water onto her face. Taking a deep breath, she savored the refreshing sensation, then sat back on her heels. Though they remained in the shade most of the morning, the late-May day had already heated to a roasting temperature, and she was drenched in sweat. The dense and heavy air coupled with the thickening cloud cover threatened an evening thunderstorm. Margaret took one last sip of the cool water before dipping a pot full to take back to the others where they had stopped for a quick midday respite in the shade of a grove of trees.

She found all as she had left it. Iain and Muireall sat eating jerked venison. Margaret turned to her husband, but he did not look in her direction. She frowned. Despite the sweet moments they had shared the night before, tension seemed stretched between them today, with Iain struggling to meet her gaze. Why was it that she and her husband could not seem to share a single intimate moment without taking a step backward?

She set the pot on the ground and stood before Iain with her hands on her hips. He chewed on his jerky for a minute before he looked up at her. Her husband motioned for her to take a seat on the log beside him, then held out a piece of the jerked meat for her. She accepted it and settled beside him. "When we're ready to go, we should return to that rock outcropping we saw about a mile back."

Margaret's brows pulled even closer together. Backtrack? An entire mile?

"Go back?" Muireall's incredulous voice echoed her own thoughts.

Iain sighed and glanced at the darkening sky before he turned to Margaret. When he did, his pale-blue gaze was almost pleading. "I am sorry. I thought we would find a better place to make camp for the night if we pushed a bit farther, but we need to take shelter from this storm."

Margaret nodded. "Yer right."

"Um, um…" The nervousness in Muireall's voice did not align with the incredulity of the moment before. Margaret turned to find her with eyes wide, her arm stretched out, pointing to something to their left.

Margaret followed the direction she indicated and gasped. A coyote stood less than a stone's throw away. Before she could react, Iain's arm shot out in front of her. When the animal wobbled forward as though it had imbibed moonshine, Margaret's heart kicked into double time.

Rabies.

Instinctively, she climbed backward over the log, keeping her movements slow and measured. She inched closer to Muireall, who sat frozen on her rock, while Iain lifted the rifle he kept at his side. The coyote took another step, then stumbled sideways several paces. Margaret took Muireall by her shoulders and coaxed her up and away as the animal turned in a drunken circle.

"Turn away, ladies," Iain rumbled as he aimed his rifle.

Margaret's chest squeezed at the thought of what had to be

done. She placed an arm around Muireall's shoulder and angled her away. Margaret jerked at the loud crack of the rifle, while Muireall let out a little whimper.

Iain had hit his mark. The rabid animal lay dead and bleeding on the ground. Still, her husband crept closer to ensure the coyote was dead. Once convinced, he turned toward her, his gaze meeting hers. A wrinkle cut across his forehead. With quick strides, he covered the distance between them.

"I will stay an' tend to the animal. We cannae risk scavengers discoverin' the body an' the disease spreadin'. Ye an' Muireall need to start back to the rock outcropping. Do ye remember where it was?"

"I believe so," she replied, sounding surer than she felt.

A bolt of lightning cut a jagged path across the sky. Margaret's scalp prickled.

Iain groaned and moved nearer. Placing a hand on her arm, he looked back the way they had come. "Take Goldie. I will meet ye there."

Margaret nodded, but it was as though a vice squeezed her heart. While she had barely known Iain for two weeks, the thought of parting ways pained her. But another bright flash of lightning lit the sky, and thunder boomed overhead.

Suddenly, Iain's gaze darkened. Leaning in, he pressed an urgent kiss to her lips. Then he pulled back and gently pushed her arm. "Go," he all but growled.

Margaret turned and grabbed Muireall's arm, ushering her to where the mare stood grazing on a patch of grass beside the creek. Loosening her reins from the tree branch where she was tied, Margaret led them back the way they had come. No sooner than their journey had begun than cool rain dropped onto her head and face. Picking up the pace, she led Muireall back over the countryside, praying they would actually find the location Iain spoke of.

∼

*B*y the time Iain finished the task of burying the diseased animal, the rain fell in thick, driving sheets, and thunder rumbled with every passing second. He wiped a hand over his face, but it did little to help, for more water fell in place of what he wiped away.

Throwing the short-handled shovel over his shoulder, he started in the direction he had sent the women. New streams of water ran in rivulets down the hillside as he hurried across the rain-soaked earth. He moved farther uphill, away from the creek at the bottom, since it would swell outside of its bounds with the new influx of water. Had Margaret done the same? Had they made it to the destination, or had they located the stone ledge at all? Iain shook his head and kept moving. He could not allow such thoughts to steal his focus as he picked his way over branch and rock.

Still, it was as though a dark cloud had gathered in his mind. His life had been one marked with tragedy. His father's drunkenness, his mother's death, his own drunkenness, and that one fateful night that had caused him to leave the colonies and never look back. Not to mention the Chickamauga raid that had happened on his watch, when he had lost his ear and the lives of over thirty souls traveling westward.

And now…when he had finally found a wife, someone who seemed to actually care for him, would he lose both her and her sister in a tide? The thought drove Iain farther, faster. He had to make it to the sisters before anything happened to them.

But dusk had fallen. And the harder the rain fell, the muddier the ground became. White lightning lit up the sky as Iain slipped and nearly went down. He jabbed the short shovel into the ground to keep him from slipping down the steep terrain, then kept it at his side as he continued to push on. Over roots and under grapevines. Around flailing branches.

With another strike of lightning, Margaret's countenance flashed into his mind. The image of the fear that had traveled over her face just before he sent her on her way haunted him. If he had sent her to her death...

Again, he pushed the thought from his mind and kept going. He could not let that happen. Just then, his foot snagged on a root and brought him crashing to the muddy earth. "Ah," he cried out as his right arm came down on the shovel. Metal bit into his flesh. He rolled onto his side and grasped his forearm. Without looking down, he could feel the ripped material and marred flesh under his fingertips.

Groaning, Iain sat up and pulled his shirt off over his head. The drenched garment would do little to staunch the bleeding, but it was all he had. So, with a grimace, he wrapped the wound as tightly as he could and tied the soaked sleeves. Then, keeping the arm held tight to his bare torso and leaving the shovel behind, he pressed on.

But with each step, it seemed his feet became more like lead and his bandage turned darker and darker. Leaning against the trunk of a tall oak, Iain stopped to gain his bearings. Surveying the darkening scenery around him, lit by brief flashes of lightning that played tricks with his vision, he did not recognize where he was. Rain continued to pour down his face, and thunder rumbled through his head. Had he not yet made it to the stone outcropping? Or had he gone past it? He turned to gaze back in the direction he had come, but the land looked as foreign to him as it did the other way. A lump formed in Iain's throat as a sensation of utter helplessness washed over him.

He fell to his knees.

Lord, I know I turned me back on Ye an' have not prayed as I should have. But I could really use Yer help right now.

He wasn't sure why he prayed to a God that had abandoned him so many times before, a God who had dealt him such a nasty hand at life. But he could think of nothing else to do.

I am lost, an' I dinnae know what to do or where to go. Lord, please help me find Margaret. Ye only just brought her to me. Please dinnae take her from me yet. Or I from her. Please, Lord, dinnae leave the women out here in the wilderness without a guide. I promise Ye, Lord. If Ye will only let me find her, if Ye will give us this chance to be together, I will commit to her an' the vow I have made. I will try to be the faithful, lovin' husband that she needs an' deserves. Please, Lord, I ask only for this one chance.

Iain opened his eyes. With rain still pelting his face in heavy droplets, he remained clueless on which direction to proceed. Had God abandoned him for good?

But as he waited there on his knees, the rain slowly started to lighten. The rumbles of thunder grew more distant, and a single ray of late-afternoon sunshine pierced through the clouds to shine onto the earth.

With the hope of that ray seeping into his soul, he stood and trudged toward it. It was like an invisible beacon, drawing him. As the land rose, he could see over the next small rise to where the sun landed on the earth—atop a rock outcropping with a golden mare standing at its edge. Iain almost hit his knees again, this time from relief. But he plowed forward.

As he neared, a figure stepped out into the sun. Margaret. Behind her, a rainbow splashed the sky as the last of the day's sunshine invaded the now-misting rain. His heart gave a leap, and for the first time in years, real hope stirred within his soul.

Margaret turned as he approached, and her mouth dropped open. "Iain!" Without hesitation, she ran over the uneven terrain to him. After slamming into him with a grateful embrace, she pulled back and looked at his arm. "What happened to ye?"

"Accident with the shovel." His voice came out gravelly.

Worry darkened the blue of her eyes. She wrapped her hands around his good arm and hauled him toward the outcropping. "Muireall, lay out the furs," she called. "An' I need a sewin' kit."

A smile tugged at the corner of his mouth even as he thought he might fall over. His wife, taking charge in the face of disaster. Despite his unworthiness, the Lord had put him in excellent hands.

~

*A*fter helping her husband lower himself onto the furs, Margaret scurried over to collect a pot and rushed to the creek's edge. She frowned at the muddied, churning water but dipped the vessel in, anyway. Without having removed the bandage yet, she could not know if the wound would be cleaner with or without the water. But she would soon find out.

Within moments, she was back by Iain's side, unwrapping his crude bandage. She cringed at the sight of the marred flesh. Unfortunately, blood, dirt, and debris all smeared across his arm, including the wound. She would have to attempt to clean it as best she could. And there was no time to boil the water if dry wood could even be found. Her husband had lost much too much blood already, if the paleness of his face was any indicator. Or the way he slumped wearily onto the furs. Even now, he laid with his other arm across his eyes as she set to work washing the wound.

Finally, satisfied that it was as clean as could be under the circumstances, she threaded a needle. Her heart beat faster than she would have liked. Hopefully, her hand would remain steadier than it felt. Though, she was not sure if the trembling was from the nearness of her shirtless husband or the gravity of the situation.

Turning so that she sat beside his head, but far enough away that she could rest his arm across her lap, she settled with her legs tucked under her and forced herself to make the first stitch. Iain grunted, revealing that he was indeed awake. Margaret paused, then continued, stitch after stitch. The long gash took over twenty stitches to close before she wrapped it with a proper bandage, torn from a cotton sheet she had brought from home. Iain made no more sound until she was completely finished. Then he moved his uninjured arm from his face so that he could examine her work. As she replaced her needle and thread in her sewing kit, his weary but grateful gaze landed on her face.

"Thank ye, lass," he whispered huskily.

Margaret offered him a smile as she forced back the tears that threatened behind her eyes. Lord willing, her husband would be all right. She brushed her fingers across his forehead before she brought her hand to the side of his face. To her surprise, Iain leaned into her touch, even turning his head to press a kiss to the palm of her hand. Warm tingles passed through her hand and traveled to the rest of her body. She leaned forward and kissed his forehead in return.

She wanted to express how grateful she was that God brought him back to her, how fear had gripped her like nothing she had ever known when she thought she might never see him again. But out of fear that she would push him away, she held her tongue on the matter.

Instead, she addressed the situation at hand. "We will camp here for the night so that ye can rest an' regain ye strength. Go ahead an' rest a bit, an' I will make a broth in a while." She rubbed her fingers over the side of his face once more before she started to move away.

"Wait." He grabbed her hand. "Only if ye rest here with me for a bit." He patted the fur next to him. Margaret glanced up at Muireall, who sat wide-eyed at the rear of the cave, then back to her husband.

"I will not fall asleep," she told Muireall before moving to join Iain. Warm prickles covered her skin as she lowered her face to rest on his bare chest.

But as she settled in, so perfectly content and comfortable in the crook of Iain's arm, she was not sure she could keep her word. Exhaustion from their travels and the day's ordeals weighed heavily on her. And when Iain's breaths became even and relaxed, they were like a lullaby to her ears. How, in the middle of so much bad, could there be so much good?

CHAPTER 8

When Margaret reached the Rolling Fork River the next day with her husband and sister, the river had swelled outside of its bounds due to the recent rains. Aptly named, the greenish-brown water rolled and churned past them.

Margaret frowned and looked up at Iain, whose face was still paler than she would have preferred for travel. His blue eyes were narrowed as he surveyed and assessed. Lines formed at the corners of his lips where they turned downward.

"Are ye sure we should not wait a day for the river to recede?" she asked.

The creases on his face deepened before he turned to her. "Not if more rain comes."

At his reply, Margaret glanced heavenward. For the second day, thick cloud cover hung overhead, casting a gloominess over their journey. "True." She looked back to the river, unease swirling in her middle. Though it provided the gateway to Muireall's safety, the swollen water presented hazards that weighed heavily on her.

"If I go across first, I can guide the mare across with ye an' Muireall."

Margaret's gaze snapped to her husband's face. "Yer in no condition to swim across alone." Her heart kicked up a notch, and breathing became difficult.

Iain turned and brought his hands to the sides of her face. His thumb caressed her cheek as he gave her a pointed look. "There is no other way."

Tears pressed at the backs of Margaret's eyes, but she refused to let them fall. Blinking them back, she nodded. Iain leaned in and brought his lips to hers. Pressing onto her toes, Margaret eagerly returned the gesture, deepening the kiss at a tiny voice telling her it could be their last.

Iain pulled away and set to work. Untying the rope from where it was coiled against the side of the saddle, he tied one end to the saddle. Then, walking a short distance down the river, he waded in. Margaret's throat constricted as Muireall stepped up next to her and drew a quavering breath to speak.

"He cannae swim across. He does not have the strength. What if he drowns an' leaves us with no guide?" Her voice rose with panic as she spoke, and Margaret's heart squeezed tighter.

Did her sister not realize that she knew the risks all too well? Did she not understand that, to Margaret, Iain was so much more than a guide? Or that this was a sacrifice they were willing to make for Muireall's safety?

She ground her teeth to keep the questions from tumbling out, her gaze not wavering from her husband as he waded deeper and deeper into the murky water. A cold chill passed over her as the depths rose to his neck. Then Iain surged forward, and she knew his feet had left the bottom. His arms began to cut through the water, pulling him through the deepest part. Margaret gripped Goldie's reins tighter.

But Iain grew farther away from her and closer to the far shore. Before she knew it, he was back in chest-deep water and making his exit. A sigh of relief left her. Iain strode across the shore and anchored the rope around a tree before he nodded at her, indicating that it was their turn.

She returned his nod before turning to Muireall. Her sister's blue eyes held a healthy dose of fear, but the set of her jaw showed she was ready to proceed. A tiny amount of the tension coiled within Margaret eased. "Ye will take the far side of the mare. Ye can hold onto the rope, an' Goldie's body will keep ye from driftin' downstream."

When Muireall agreed, Margaret stepped up beside the mare. Lifting her chin, she asked the animal to walk forward. Together, their feet dipped into the cool depths. Holding tightly to the rope, she moved deeper, the waters rising up her legs under her skirts.

Breaking her concentration, Muireall's voice drifted over Goldie's shoulder, wavering as she recited, "'The Lord is my shepherd; I shall not want. He maketh me to lie down in green pastures: he leadeth me beside the still waters. He restoreth my soul: he leadeth me in the paths of righteousness for his name's sake.'"

A calm likened to that of joy entered Margaret's soul as she continued forward, joining her sister in saying, "'Yea, though I walk through the valley of the shadow of death, I will fear no evil: for thou art with me; thy rod and thy staff they comfort me. Thou preparest a table before me in the presence of mine enemies: thou anointest my head with oil; my cup runneth over. Surely goodness and mercy shall follow me all the days of my life: and I will dwell in the house of the Lord for ever.'"

Keeping her eyes focused on Iain on the far shore, she continued to whisper the words over and over, even as the ground disappeared from beneath her. Though her petticoats weighed her down, the current tugging at them, her grip remained tight on the rope as the mare surged steadily forward.

Finally, everyone's feet were on solid ground. As she quickly squeezed the water from her dress, a smile spread over her face when Iain's boots appeared in her field of vision. When she straightened, her heart lightened, for he, too, wore a small smile across his face as he brought her close for a wet embrace. Warmth spread through her as he pressed a quick kiss to her lips. She had to admit, she took great pleasure in the affection he had shown since he found them under the stone outcropping. Maybe, just maybe, the ordeal had helped him come to realize his feelings for her?

~

As Iain lowered the saddle to the ground later that day, he swayed, black dots swimming in his vision. Putting a hand to the base of the maple beside him, he steadied himself and waited for the sensation to pass. The river crossing had stolen more of the precious strength he had left than he'd realized. However, camp had been established, and while he watered the mare, Margaret had already set to making a broth.

The corner of his mouth tipped up as he led Goldie down to a nearby creek. Though his wife was caring and spirited, and he now found her quite beautiful, she was also rather skilled at burning food. He could count on the meat in the soup having a charred taste and a chewy texture. Still, her efforts were admirable.

Actually, his wife was much more than admirable. After committing himself to their marriage, his eyes had been opened even further to her wonderful qualities. Iain splashed more water upon his face despite the fact that his clothes were still drying. Summer was pushing spring out of the way, and the day had proved hot and muggy.

Finally, the mare had drank her fill, and he could return to the wife that seemed to fill his thoughts lately. With more rain impending, they had made a shelter under a grove of pines, tying more branches together to form a lean-to underneath their protection. He approached their camp when a sound stopped him in his tracks. Margaret's melodic voice drifted to him through the branches, the words to a hymn on her lips. Creeping closer so that he could observe unbeknownst to her, he peered through the trees to where she sat merrily stirring a pot of broth.

Muireall sat off to the side, embroidering, as usual. His mouth pulled into a frown. Though, his Margaret never seemed to care that she carried all the responsibility between the two. Always, his wife was the one to tend to the chores. Likely, she had done so all her life, stepping up when someone was needed. His heart swelled, carrying him closer to her.

At the snapping of a twig, her gaze came up to meet his, and the music died.

"Dinnae stop," he said huskily as he entered the makeshift lean-to, taking a seat on the ground next to her.

She sent a shy smile his way before she resumed the lyrics, enchanting him so that he relaxed fully. He could easily fall asleep listening to the blessed sound. But that could wait until after dinner. For his wife ladled a steaming portion of meat and broth into his tin cup and handed it over. His stomach grumbled as he took it from her.

Margaret stopped her singing and frowned at him. "After ye eat, ye need to rest."

Iain nodded. He must look even worse than he felt. Though a good meal and a night's rest should be all he needed.

~

Margaret blinked awake, the steady patter of rainfall meeting her ears. A smile spread across her face at the peaceful sound. No other sounds could be heard aside from the breathing of the two people she cherished most in the world. Though, as she listened, she noted a difference in the breathing of the man resting behind her. Rather than soft and shallow, his breaths were oddly pronounced. She looked over her shoulder, and her heart nearly stopped.

Iain laid with an arm stretched above him, his mouth agape and his body glistening with sweat. His chest rose and fell with each labored breath. *No, no, no.* Margaret laid the back of her hand on his forehead. Fever.

What had her mother done for fevers when they were growing up? A growl of frustration rose from her chest when she could not recollect any remedies. There were vague memories, though, of a cold compress being pressed to her forehead when she was younger.

After leaping up, she hurried to the saddlebags, where she withdrew a dish rag before dashing through the rain down to the creek. She plunged the fabric in the cold water, then turned and ran back to their pine-bough shelter, where she knelt and placed it on his forehead. Her heart ached to see him in such a state, his hair disheveled and damp with sweat.

Suddenly, a memory came flooding back to her. Feverfew tea—as he had made her for her injury. Named as it was, could it have the same healing effects on a fever? Margaret scurried over to where Muireall still slept and shook her sister.

"Wh-what is it?" Muireall blinked and looked around.

"I need ye to keep an eye on Iain. Keep the cold compress on his forehead wet, an' start a fire so I can make tea when I return."

"Where?" Her brows scrunched, but Margaret did not wait around to hear the remainder of her sister's question. She dashed out into the soft rain in search of the precious plant that might be the medicine her husband needed.

Scouring the area nearest the camp first, she searched for the plants that resembled those Iain had used. When that did not yield any results, she set out across the countryside, searching one hillside, then the next. However, she was careful to keep her bearings with regard to the camp's location. After searching in every direction to no avail, she slapped her hands against her sides and glanced at the sky.

Cool rain fell against her face, only deepening her frustration. The cold compress...she had not searched on the other side of the creek. Margaret turned and ran in the opposite direction, past camp. Sliding the last few feet to the water's edge, she tromped through and started her search anew. *Please, Lord*, she begged silently.

Finally, the earth gave way to a meadow where the plant's herbaceous aroma wafted up to her. Kneeling to check the leaves, she offered a quick prayer of thanks when she noted them to be the shape she sought. After gathering up as many as she could carry, she turned and sprinted back to camp, slipping and sliding as she went.

Her mouth fell open as she entered the lean-to. Muireall had started a nice little fire and sat beside Iain's head, her lips drawn tight. She glanced up at Margaret's arrival. "I just wetted the rag again. An' I brought up a pot of the spring water so we can keep it damp."

Dropping her bundles of feverfew, Margaret went to her sister and wrapped her in a quick hug. "Thank ye," she whispered, her throat tight with emotion. Then she set to work on the tea.

The two of them shared no other words as they entered into a silent arrangement of caring for Iain together. While Margaret prepared the tea and coaxed what she could past her husband's lips, Muireall continued to make sure the compress stayed cool. Then Muireall assumed the duty of preparing a broth for them while Margaret tended to the compress, fetching another pot of cold water.

As Margaret trudged back up the hillside from the creek, she thanked her heavenly Father for her sister's attentive aid.

Though worry still knotted Margaret's stomach, Muireall's assistance eased a tiny portion of the burden from her shoulders. While Margaret could not dismiss the idea that her sister might be acting solely out of fear of being left alone and unguided in the wilderness if Iain perished, Muireall did appear genuinely concerned. And she would not question her sister's motives, especially when Muireall was stepping up in a way she never had before—right when it was most needed.

Hours later, Margaret leaned against the pine closest to Iain while Muireall read from their mother's Bible. "'Fear thou not; for I am with thee: be not dismayed; for I am thy God: I will strengthen thee; yea, I will help thee; yea, I will uphold thee with the right hand of my righteousness.'"

The words were like a balm to Margaret's weary soul, and she lifted her millionth prayer of the day, asking God to heal her husband. The day had long ago turned to night, and she could barely keep her eyes open, but still Iain's fever raged. Each time she touched his burning skin and felt the thick sweat, worry swirled in her stomach, and she would say another prayer.

Finally, Muireall approached her. "Ye need to get some rest. I will keep an eye on him an' wake ye in a few hours."

Margaret looked into her sister's eyes, which were a darker shade than hers and completely blue. Today, they held a compassion and understanding that was nearly her undoing. Muireall's pale hand came out to grip hers, causing tears to well in her eyes. She did not want to rest, and she probably could not sleep even if she tried. But still, she went over and curled up next to Iain's side. She gripped the edge of his shirt as she closed her eyes and began another prayer.

～

*I*ain slowly pried his eyes open to the early-morning sun that filtered into their makeshift shelter. His throat felt as though it was full of wood shavings. Glancing around, he found Margaret curled by his side and Muireall slumped against a tree trunk with a Bible laid open in her lap, both asleep. How odd, though. Had Muireall fallen asleep keeping watch?

Not wanting to wake either woman, he managed to slowly sit up. Looking around, he found a cup and a pot of water, so he dipped a portion and took small sips until his throat no longer felt quite so rough. Then, realizing he needed to tend to matters, he forced his body from the ground so that he could step outside the shelter and relieve himself. The morning was lovely, though warm, with a light breeze that kept the air comfortable and promised a pleasant day for travel.

Stretching his aching limbs, Iain soaked in the sunshine a moment longer before he ducked back into the shelter, where he was greeted by a wide-eyed Margaret.

"Iain?" The worry and fear in her voice brought him quickly to her side.

"Aye, it is me, lass." He brushed the hair from her cheek.

As though she could not quite believe he was well again, she placed her hands on each side of his face, then pressed a cool hand to his forehead. "Yer fever broke." A smile blossomed across her face, and tears filled her eyes.

"Aye," he agreed as she threw her arms around his neck. He pulled her into his embrace and cradled her in his lap. "Thanks to the attentiveness of ye an' yer sister. How many days have passed?"

"Two," she said, and her mouth pressed into a line. Worry reflected in her eyes once more.

"But I am well now," he reminded her as he brought his forehead down to hers.

"Aye." She wrapped her arms tighter around his neck and pressed her body closer to his.

Thankful for the opportunity to hold Margaret once again, Iain curled her in tight against him, her smaller body melding perfectly with his. He pressed kisses to her hair and forehead until she lifted her face. Then he bent to cover her mouth with his, savoring the way she so ardently responded, her fingers pressing into his back. He kissed her deeply and wholly, gratefulness abounding.

But before anything could go further, Iain gently set her aside. Then he crooked a finger under her chin and lifted her gaze to his. "Next time we are alone," he promised.

Her eyes widened a fraction before a beautiful blush colored her cheeks. Oh, why had he balked at fully committing to her before now? Romancing one's wife was sweet, tantalizing fun.

A stirring to his left brought him and Margaret from their own little world. Muireall pulled herself from the awkward, slumped position she had fallen asleep in. Closing the Bible, she looked around. Her eyes widened as they landed on him sitting beside her sister. Then she smiled a genuine smile, the first he had ever seen grace her face. "Yer fever broke?" Muireall glanced between him and Margaret.

Margaret nodded profusely, again on the verge of tears as she went to her sister. Iain cocked his head as the two shared a meaningful embrace. Maybe the Lord had used his ordeal for good between the two sisters?

CHAPTER 9

Inside the gates of Fort Harrod, excited anticipation or perhaps nervousness thrummed through Margaret's body, making it difficult to stand still. But she kept her feet firmly planted as she took in the interior of the massive structure. While a tall log wall formed all four sides, the corners held fortified buildings with larger tops protruding outside the walls. From the outside, it had appeared much as she would have imagined a log castle would have, with corner spires. But those fortified sections allowed for gun ports and lookouts.

Meanwhile, inside the fort was an entire town with everything a person could need. A blacksmith, farm animals, and crops could all be spotted at first glance. At the back of the fort stood a long line of small cabins. Though the abundance of green inside was different than Margaret would have imagined, one could not ignore the great wall that surrounded them on all sides. Suddenly feeling like a caged animal, Margaret glanced at Muireall. Her sister could definitely find safety here.

Margaret had imagined she would feel some sort of sense of accomplishment or completion of their journey upon arrival.

But in many ways, their journey had just begun. Now that they had arrived, they would begin their lives anew. What might life look like moving forward? In fact, where would they even lay their heads that night? Suddenly, she found herself looking at Iain.

As he glanced down at her, the same questions filled his eyes. And maybe even a darker storm? A cold chill swept through her, but she told herself it was only the uncertainty that caused her to be so apprehensive.

When a group of men approached, Iain stepped forward to meet with them and, hopefully, discuss their arrangements. Margaret stepped closer to her sister.

Muireall's eyes fixed on her, filled with wonder. A grin lifted the corners of her pink lips. "This is incredible. There is a whole world inside here."

Margaret smiled in return. "It is somethin'." It was fascinating and daunting at once to consider that most of the people before them lived the majority of their entire lives within the confines of the fort. Even the settlements outside the gate looked to the fort for protection. Would there be a place for her and Iain there? Where they could breathe?

But what of Muireall? Margaret would only feel Muireall was truly safe if she lived within the walls. At the moment, her sister seemed mesmerized at the thought, the summer breeze tugging her raven hair loose and swirling it around her awestruck porcelain face. But would she be willing to live separately from Margaret and Iain? Margaret frowned as a whole new set of worries and considerations swirled within her mind.

Thankfully, Iain returned then with a man who was several inches shorter than him but whose shoulders were broader. Despite the heat, he wore a dark cotton vest over his linen shirt, and his hair was pulled back and tied with a strip of leather. "Margaret, Muireall, this is Mr. Harrod."

The man's smile was broad and jovial as he greeted them.

"You can call me James. So nice to meet you ladies. Ann will be glad to hear of your arrival. She is always thankful for the presence of more women about the place."

"Nice to meet ye as well." Margaret shook his proffered hand.

"Now, as I was telling your husband…"

A small thrill at hearing the handsome man beside her called her husband caused pride to surge in her chest. Margaret chanced a quick glance at Iain, a smile tugging at her lips. But his expression was unreadable as he watched Mr. Harrod.

"You are in luck. We recently had a family move out, and there is a cabin available here in the fort. Back in the far corner." He motioned to the right, near the looming lookout tower.

Margaret swallowed and resisted the urge to turn and flee. Instead, as Mr. Harrod led them toward their new home, her feet moved obediently forward. Iain stepped up beside her, and the hand he placed on the small of her back reassured her. Goldie followed along beside Iain as Mr. Harrod continued to drone on about how they would be expected to contribute in some way to life in the fort, but Margaret found herself unable to focus on his words. For she could not tear her gaze away from cabin after cabin they passed that were built in the exact same size, shape, and fashion. Their sloping roofs were highest in the back and slanted forward.

Finally, they stopped outside their new home. Margaret had not felt this much unrest when her family had left the colonies to move into the wilderness of Kentucky. Instead, when circumstances had been far more uncertain, she had felt only excitement at the opportunity that lay before them. Trying to channel some of that emotion now, for Muireall's sake, she mounted the steps and walked into the square building.

But inside, Margaret's stomach dropped. The cabin's interior seemed even smaller than it had on the outside—only about half the size of the home they had left less than two weeks prior. There was one large bed with a trundle below and a stone fireplace. A small hutch sat in the back right corner behind a tiny rocking chair that seemed barely large enough for a grown person. Lastly, a small square table took up the front corner. The three of them would barely be able to turn around without bumping into one another.

"Cozy," Muireall offered with a grin, suddenly the optimist of the bunch.

"Aye," Margaret agreed. And though she attempted a smile of her own, the word came out tight.

"Well, I will leave you to settle in." Mr. Harrod's words drifted to her from the doorway.

"Thank ye." Iain's voice rumbled behind Margaret, the familiar sound providing her some comfort.

With one last glance around the room, she raised her chin. If this was to be their new home, she had work to do. Stalking back out of the cabin, she strode to Goldie's side and began to remove items from the mare's load.

"I will unpack an' put our belongings away," she advised Iain as he came out to assist.

"I will tend to the mare." He gazed across the fort as he no doubt wondered exactly how and where that would take place as well.

Margaret sighed as she carried an armload of items into their home. There would simply be an adjustment period as they learned their new surroundings. Perhaps they could find a sense of community that would ease the transition?

~

*A*pprehension tingled up Iain's spine as he walked back to the cabin after settling Goldie into her temporary home in the animal corral. The poor mare had eyed the sheep warily, blowing out loud puffs of air as she attempted to determine if they were friend or foe. Iain could relate. Though they were no longer at risk of Indian attack, the surroundings seemed as foreign and unsettling to him as they had the mare.

"Lord, please keep me from temptation."

He had left the eastern colonies for one reason—to remove himself from the presence of the drink that had nearly consumed him as a younger man. But this settlement reminded him too much of those towns where one could always find strong liquor. Though Iain liked to think that the years had made him stronger, a deep-seated fear lingered, deep down, that he was still no different from the father he had loathed. Would his care for Margaret, if not his weak faith, be enough to help him resist temptation?

A sudden, powerful urge to be near the wife he was coming to love dearly caused him to jog back to the cabin, ignoring the questioning glances thrown his way as he went. The door stood open, and both women startled at the sound Iain's boots made on the steps. Margaret placed a hand on her chest as she released a breath, her mouth curving into the first genuine smile he had seen since their arrival. The sight calmed his nerves but sent butterflies swirling in his stomach. Ones that made him want to march across the miniscule room and sweep her into a kiss. But with Muireall present, he opted to turn around one of the chairs from the tiny table so that he could be near Margaret as she bent over a pan, warming meat over the fire.

Muireall, on the other hand, seemed to be an excited flurry of activity. While Margaret cooked, Muireall unloaded the saddlebags and packs, checking in with her sister on where various items should go. Not that there was much of a place for anything. What a shame circumstances had forced him to take the women from their larger cabin. But at least they were safe from attack. And surely, this would not be their home forever?

Once the conflicts in Kentucky had settled down, the world outside the fort might be safe enough for them to start afresh. But when would that be?

Suddenly, Margaret was by his side, a hand on his shoulder. "Were ye able to get Goldie settled?" She slid a plate of sizzling, albeit burnt, venison onto the table next to him, pulling him from his thoughts.

"Aye."

Though two sides of the table were pushed against the wall and there were only two straight-backed chairs, Margaret placed two more plates on the table, petticoats swishing with each step. Iain stood to retrieve another seat, colliding with his wife as she turned. As her vibrant eyes came up to his, her lips parted in surprise. He grinned. Maybe it would not be so terrible living in such close quarters?

He bent and stole a quick, sweet kiss before he grabbed the rocking chair and moved it over to the corner of the table for Margaret. Taking her hand, he drew her into the seat next to him. The feel of her hand in his and the gentle smile she sent his way offered the reassurance he had needed.

Bowing his head, he offered grace, thanking the Lord for the food before them and safe arrival at their destination. Then he asked God to lead them in the days that came, for His guidance in their lives. Margaret's hand squeezed his tighter, revealing that she, too, held similar concerns. Finally, he asked the Lord to take their worries from them and help them to trust in Him. For without the Lord's path and guidance, they would be lost.

～

*M*argaret straightened from where she was bent over harvesting spring cabbage and wiped sweat from her forehead with the back of her sleeve. The June sun beat down on her and several other women as they worked in the two garden plots. They had spent the morning planting additional crops and now were tending to the early harvest. Not a single ripe fruit or ready vegetable could be missed when there were so many mouths to feed. Margaret was thankful, though, that the gardens needed constant tending. For her, it was the perfect excuse to spend time outdoors while still contributing to the success of the settlement.

She stood and made her way down to the pole beans, where the first few beans were coming ready. Still small, they could use another day or two. Then, though she knew there was nothing else ready, she started her daily walk through the gardens, weaving in and out of the rows. That was, until she turned down the row where Betty Davidson and Mary Coulter stood chatting beside the tomato plants.

"Margaret!" Betty cheered as though they had not seen one another only twenty minutes prior.

Before Margaret could come up with a reason to excuse herself, Betty came forward and took her arm. She ushered her forward to join the conversation.

"Jack, you stop pinching your sister," Mary called out to the two young children playing nearby. Blond-headed Jack frowned and trudged after his sister, whose braids bounced against her back as she skipped away.

The woman turned back to them with pinched lips and raised brows. From what little Margaret had learned in their first week at the fort, Mary was not near as friendly as Betty, though the two were fast friends. As though to prove her point, Mary looked Margaret up and down with dark, piercing eyes and her mouth pinching even further. "So when are you goin' to have yourself some young 'uns?"

Margaret frowned and bit her tongue. When they lived in the bustling Harrodstown and could not get a single moment alone in the cramped quarters of their cabin, how were she and

Iain supposed to have children? Instead, she offered the woman a forced smile. "When the good Lord sees fit."

While she offered no reply, Mary's nose rose higher in the air, as though she had smelled something foul. Betty, however, gasped and clasped a hand over her mouth. "Oh, I hope He does soon! Would you and your husband not make just the cutest babies? With his bright blue eyes and your thick, beautiful locks."

A genuine smile broke out across Margaret's face as she turned to the tall woman to her left. Her hand went to her hair, which was falling from the knot she had tried to tame it in that morning. Wisps stuck to her face and neck, plastered there by sweat. Not once in her life had she ever considered her hair beautiful. "Why, thank ye, Betty. I am glad ye believe so."

"Mhmm." A sound of disapproval came from Mary's direction, and it was all Margaret could do not to send a glare at the woman.

"Well, I have a lot to do, so I suppose I will leave ye ladies to it," she excused herself.

"See you tomorrow," Betty called after her as she exited the garden.

Margaret angled back only long enough to give her a polite wave before she turned up the worn path to the cabins. Knowing exactly where she would find Muireall, she dashed up the steps of the first dwelling and peeked into the open door. Her sister sat rocking beside the hearth opposite a wrinkled, gray-headed woman whose eyes crinkled as she peered down at her needlework.

"Come on in, dearie," Mrs. Petunia Allen called without looking up, though her back was turned to Margaret.

As Margaret stepped into the cabin, Muireall glanced up and smiled broadly. She dropped her sewing in the basket beside her and rushed to Margaret's side. Taking the basket from Margaret, Muireall settled it on the little corner table, which was much the same as their own. "Oh, Margaret, ye should see the fabric we dyed this mornin'. It came out the most beautiful orange color that would look absolutely wonderful on ye. Ye have to let me make ye a dress out of it."

"Of course." Margaret could not possibly decline her sister's offer when the girl had found such a passion and place in her short time at the fort. Unlike Margaret, her skills with needle and thread had earned her a welcome place among the women. And she could easily contribute her services to those around her. Instead of being despondent and petulant, her sister was now lively and happy.

"Good." Muireall grinned at her before she practically floated back to the rocking chair.

Margaret kept her feet glued, as out of place in the cabin with Muireall and Petunia as she had been in the garden with the judgmental Mary. As Muireall took up her sewing, the tug of thread through fabric and the rhythmic creaking of the rocking chairs were the only sounds.

Finally, Petunia spoke up, drawing Margaret's attention. "I thought I might keep yer sister for the night." The woman did not look up but kept rocking, and kept pushing her needle through the white fabric in her lap.

Thankfully, Muireall filled the gap of information the elderly lady had left. "Aye. Mrs. Brown is expecting twins any day now, an' I am helpin' to make their gowns." Again, her sister's face glowed. Joy spread through Margaret at the sight, easing her discomfort.

"What a blessin'. I am sure Iain an' I will manage alone for one night." As the words tumbled out of her mouth, realization dawned. A giddy, excited joy spread up through her middle and made her cheeks heat as she suppressed a grin. And as she turned to collect her basket from the table, she noted that Petunia's own mouth was curved in a knowing smile as she continued sewing and rocking. That sly woman.

Margaret scurried down the steps and along the path to her cabin. If she hurried, she might have time to freshen up and prepare a special meal for Iain before he returned from his hunting trip with Mr. Harrod and several others. Tonight, she might finally come to know her husband in every way.

CHAPTER 10

As Margaret lay next to Iain, she could not fall asleep. Instead, she found herself staring at the ceiling in the darkness. Such a restless, confined feeling had taken root deep within her the moment she had set foot in the fort. Though, for the life of her, she could not understand why. Life was good.

Not only had Muireall found a place within the community and a deep satisfaction and joy in her work, but she had also found a close comrade in Petunia Allen. In fact, the elderly woman had asked her more than a month prior to move in with her so that no one would be bothered by their long hours of needlework. An offer which Muireall had gladly accepted. Likely, the woman was lonely, and Muireall's company brought her joy.

The arrangement worked out quite well for her and Iain also. They had finally been able to settle into a routine as a married couple. In fact, her time with her husband was one of her few joys in the day. Though none of the problems of before plagued them—there was always food in the pantry, and there were no real dangers within the fort—Margaret was more tired than ever.

She was tired of interacting with people every single time she set foot outside her door. She was tired of entertaining questions or snide remarks from the other women. And while Iain had ventured outside the fort to hunt and she to forage and gather, all was done in groups for safety.

In the fort, one was simply never alone. The only time Margaret was able to enjoy an ounce of solitude was in the cabin. And then she felt as though she might suffocate. In many ways, the fort more resembled a prison than a home.

She should be grateful that God had delivered them to such a wonderful place and provided for them. And yet, the restlessness would not still.

Finally, she threw the covers off and lit a candle. Then, taking her mother's Bible down from the mantel, she settled at the table in the corner. She flipped it open and started to read. Normally, the words would bring her peace, but now, she could not seem to focus.

A stirring across the room drew her attention, and Iain shuffled across the room to join her, his hair disheveled and his eyelids low with sleepiness. He covered a yawn as he approached, lowering himself into the other chair. "Could not sleep?"

"Nay." Margaret frowned.

Iain nodded but did not return to bed. Instead, he simply sat with her in the dark, keeping her silent company. Oddly enough, it provided more of a balm to her weary soul than the words written before her.

"Iain, does this feel like home to ye?" She finally voiced the question on her mind. Her husband's lips pressed into a line, and he was quiet for several moments before he spoke. "For over four years, I have not had a home. I have lived as a guide an' long hunter, roamin' the wilderness without a place to call home. An' even before that..." He shook his head. "I am not even sure I know what home feels like."

Iain's frown reflected the discomfort that stirred inside her. She reached out and covered her hand with his. "Moments like these, I feel at home. Here with ye in the quiet. But then I step outside, with all those people. An' the walls. An' nothin' about it feels like home."

Iain raised his brows and nodded. "It is enough to make a person lose their mind."

Margaret sighed. Though she was glad her husband could relate to her dilemma, what was there to do about it? She could not leave Muireall.

As though he read her thoughts, Iain took her hand into his and lifted it to his mouth for a kiss, sending pleasant shivers down her spine. "Margaret, I would be glad to make me home with ye wherever ye like. I know ye wanted to bring Muireall here, to keep her safe. An' more than anythin', I want to keep ye safe. But we dinnae have to make our home here."

Margaret frowned again. "It is just...when we were headed west with Pa...there was one mornin' me an' him woke early to watch the sunrise from the mountaintop. Watchin' the sky splashed with color over the rolling hills, with expanses of trees an' green in all directions, there seemed so much promise. Comin' west, there seemed so much freedom an' opportunity waitin' for us. An' I know there is bounty an' opportunity here at Fort Harrod. Muireall has found it to be so. But I dinnae feel that same way here. Not as I did at home, surrounded by hills an' hollers, waking to birds singin'."

Iain smiled as he leaned forward and took both her hands in his. "Margaret, darlin', I believe ye have just answered yer own question."

Slowly, Margaret realized what she had finally put into words. And suddenly, a deep peace abounded in her soul. More than anything, she wanted to go home. "But what about Muireall? An' the dangers?"

"Muireall has her life here. Ye can speak with her, but as difficult as it may be, it could be time for ye to part ways. Ye cannae live yer entire life for yer sister. Ye deserve a life of yer own. An' as for the danger, I dinnae know. It scares me to consider takin' ye back to where I cannae protect ye. But we can pray an' ask the Lord to protect us. An' trust in Him. In all reality, that is all any of us can do."

"True."

Iain stood and pulled her into his arms. "So have ye made a decision, Mrs. Donegal?"

Margaret grinned as warmth spread up her arms. "I believe so, me husband." She looked up into his gaze, which now blazed with heat. She could barely squeeze out her next words. "Thank ye for listenin'."

Iain's face softened, and he leaned in to press a kiss to her forehead. "Anytime, darlin'. An' I meant what I said. I would follow ye to the ends of the earth." This time, he lowered his kiss to her cheek.

Margaret nodded, the sensation of his lips lingering on her skin. She snuggled into his embrace and glanced up into his face once more. "Iain?" Her heart thudded rapidly in her chest.

"Aye?" His voice was barely more than a whisper as his fingertips drew circles on the back of her shoulder.

"I love ye."

Iain's gaze snapped up to meet hers, and his hand stilled. A mere second passed before his lips were on hers. The emotions that surged between them were enough to make her whimper. It was a tiny sound, but enough that Iain pulled back and took her face into his hands. He pressed another ardent kiss to her forehead before lowering his own head to touch hers.

"I love ye, too, Margaret," he whispered.

"Ow," Margaret complained when Muireall poked her with a pin.

"Sorry!" Her sister adjusted the pin and then came around to peer at the front of the dress, her mouth set in a frown. "Has yer bust gotten larger?"

"Not that I know of. Though me skirts have grown tighter the longer we have been here."

The regular, hearty meals were a blessing and had put some weight on both her and her sister's bones. Muireall now boasted a beautiful, womanly frame rather than being desperately thin. Did she appear the same? Margaret frowned down at the gown that was pieced together over her body as she attempted to assess her own shapeliness. Then she strained to glance behind her.

"Dinnae go wrigglin' around too much. Then ye will get poked with pins." Muireall waggled a finger at her.

Petunia hunched by the fire, where she kept an eye on the fitting while tending to the cabbage she was stewing. When she lifted the lid of the old cast-iron pot to stir its contents, Margaret had to slap a hand over her mouth to keep from losing the contents of her previous meal. Though she had never preferred the smell of cabbage, she had been pleased to eat it on plenty of occasions and had never encountered any the smell of which had made her stomach roil as it did now.

Muireall placed a hand on her shoulder, her brows lowering in concern as she peered at her. "Are ye well?"

Margaret nodded, though she did not remove her hand from her mouth as she swallowed. Taking slow, deep breaths, she glanced at the offending pot of cabbage before finally allowing her hand to fall to her side.

Petunia peered at her with a wry smile. "I believe there is

more than the good meals puttin' some weight on ye." She pointed her wooden spoon in Margaret's direction.

Margaret stared at the woman. "Wha…"

Muireall gasped beside her, both her hands going to the sides of her face as a girlish giggle escaped. Margaret glanced between the two women before she finally understood their meaning. Her mouth dropped open as her hand went to her stomach, which still seemed incredibly flat to be holding a child. And yet, it had to be true. It had been two months since her courses had come. Considering she had not felt ill or faint, as her mother had with Muireall, she had ignored that crucial sign. For fear that it might not be true.

Slowly, a smile broke out across her face as the miracle of the situation sank in. She glanced at her sister, who was still giddy with joy. Muireall threw her arms around Margaret and squeezed her in a hug that caused sweet tears to fill her eyes. "I am goin' to be an aunt."

And I am goin to be a mither.

~

*M*argaret grinned as she hovered over the spread of food on the table. Beef, carrots, green beans, and bread adorned the small wooden square. And she had not burned a single thing. Giddiness swirled inside her and made her cheeks hurt as her grin broadened even further. Her hand went to her middle once more. The perfect meal for the perfect announcement.

The smile slipped from her face, though, and her shoulders sagged under the orange fabric of her new dress. The matter of her pregnancy brought into question their impending move. Not only would the journey be arduous for a pregnant woman, but she would be abandoning all medical care and taking her child into a dangerous country. The more she considered the matter, the more she wondered if it was indeed the right decision. She would discuss the matter with Iain, and regardless of what was decided, they would trust in the Lord.

At that moment, the door swung open, and suddenly, her grin was back. Iain stopped in the doorway as he drank in the sight of her, his own mischievous grin taking shape. "A new dress?"

Despite the sweltering heat, he closed the door behind him and danced over, sweeping her close for a knee-weakening kiss. "Mmm. An' what is that delicious smell?"

Margaret ushered him over to the table without even allowing him time to clean up. "I made dinner an' did not burn one bit of it," she boasted as she bent to press a kiss to his cheek once he was seated.

"Well, 'twill be a delightful night, indeed." His blue eyes held a hint of play as he captured her gaze before lowering his head for a quick grace. Butterflies swirled in Margaret's stomach as she attempted to focus on the meal, rather than blurting her news with no preamble.

As she sliced into her beef, though, her heart sank. Though there was no char, it was horribly undercooked. Ignoring the sight that made her want to retch, she moved on to her beans and carrots. However, the vegetables were each as hard as could be. The only part of their meal that was not raw was the bread, and it was dense, not having risen as it should have. Though Iain continued to eat without complaint, tears swam in her eyes. The urge to cry only deepened as she watched her husband dutifully chew and swallow the unappetizing meal. Margaret placed her hand on his arm to stop him.

Iain glanced up. Dropping his fork onto his plate with a clatter, he took her hand in his. "What is wrong?"

That opened the floodgates. "I wanted the meal to be perfect, an' it is horrible," she sobbed. "An' yet, yer sittin' there eatin' it like the kindest, most carin' man on earth. I dinnae know what I ever did to deserve such a wonderful husband."

Iain's brows tugged together in confusion before he pulled her into his lap. "Are ye well, me wife?" Fear and compassion swam in his blue eyes.

Tears still filled her eyes as she smiled and nodded. "Better than well."

Iain's brow puckered further as he failed to follow her logic. "I am with child."

Much the opposite of how she had expected him to react, he pulled back as though he had been slapped. The color drained from his face. "Yer sure?"

Margaret shrugged a shoulder and nodded. "As best I can be."

Iain's mouth pressed into a thin line before he closed his eyes and ran a hand through his hair. A heavy sigh left his body. "I am to be a father." But his words held no joy. They were strained, if not haunted.

Margaret's heart sank, but still, she answered with a quiet, "Aye."

Iain closed his eyes for several seconds longer, and she thought he might be praying. Finally, he lifted her from his lap and settled her back into her seat. "Ye...ye will be a fine mither, Margaret." Standing over her, he squeezed her shoulder before turning away. "I'm so sorry, but I forgot a matter I needed to tend to."

He walked out the door without another word, and her heart might rip in two at the pain that lodged there. Tears welled again and spilled over onto her cheeks. Had this ruined their marriage already?

*I*ain did not know where he was going as he stepped back out into the suffocating heat that still lingered in September, but he had to go somewhere. He pulled at the collar of his linen shirt. Somewhere he could breathe. Without thinking about his steps, he followed the worn path in front of the cabins. Then, ignoring glances of passersby, he turned down the main path into the gardens. The place where his wife loved to spend her time. The wife who was now with child. Iain's breaths came in quick succession as he moved on past the gardens. He could not be a father. According to his mother, his father had turned into the monster he was only after Iain's arrival. He had resented Iain's intrusion into their life and turned to drinking and violence as a result.

Coming to the gates at the entrance of the fort, Iain turned and made his way along the wall. Anything to keep moving, to outrun the fear and panic that threatened to consume him whole. His father's same blood beat within him. What if he, too, resented his own child? What if he did not see the tiny life that sprang forth from their love as the miracle that it was?

Coming to the tree behind an animal shelter, he dropped onto the grass in front of it, his hands going into his hair. Still, his heart threatened to beat out of his chest. He had known this was a possibility, thought he was ready for it. After all, he and Margaret had found happiness. A child born of that had to be a good thing, right? And yet, it seemed as though he could not draw enough air into his lungs. So many questions tumbled through his mind.

Was the baby why Margaret had yet to speak with Muireall regarding the move? Had she changed her mind? He could not blame her if she had. They had already learned of the perils of the journey. Plus, the wilderness was no place for a child, especially in the middle of an Indian war. Iain curled his fingers tighter in his hair as he released a growl of frustration.

Suddenly, his world had been flipped upside down again. And all he wanted to do was run, run far away from his problems. Just as he had that fateful night when he almost killed a man. The thought came to Iain with stark clarity. His natural instinct was to fall right back into those old patterns.

Iain squeezed his eyes closed. No, he could not do that. No matter his fears or concerns, he could not do that to Margaret. If he truly wished to be a changed man, he had to act like one. And that meant standing beside his wife and the new life she carried within her.

After climbing to his feet, Iain strode back toward the cabin. He could not ruin the relationship they had now for fear of what might happen down the road. He had to try to be a better man, for Margaret. And for himself.

He swung the door of the cabin wide, and his heart plummeted at the sight of his wife curled on the bed, her face streaked with tears. She quickly sat up and wiped at her face. Iain rushed to her side and pulled her into his lap. Stroking her tear-stained hair, he kissed the top of her head and hugged her to him. "Margaret, ye will be a wonderful mither to this baby. An' I cannae make any guarantees, but I will try me best to be a good father. We are truly blessed, me darlin'."

Margaret looked up at him through her tears, her eyes of blue, green, and hazel tugging at his insides. "Oh, Iain, ye will be a wonderful father." She threw her arms around his neck.

If only he could believe her words. But a knot of dread still twisted in his stomach.

CHAPTER 11

Margaret paused her rocking to lift her gaze from the words printed in the Bible before her to the darkness outside the open door of their cabin. Though night had fallen some time ago, her husband had yet to return. If they still lived in the wilderness back home, she would have worried some ill fate had befallen him. But there had been no hunt today, so where could Iain be?

Standing, she returned the Bible to its place on the mantel before moving to the open doorway. She wrapped her arms around herself as she turned her gaze heavenward, to the masses of stars blinking back at her, and the bright, full moon. Though the days were still uncomfortably warm, the September nights had proven to be cool and comfortable. A breeze tugged at the strands of hair around her face and kissed her cheeks with its pleasant breath. If her husband had been home, it would have been a wonderful night for a moonlit stroll. Instead, their rabbit stew cooled over dying embers, and her only companion was the chirping of crickets.

Finally, the crunch of a rock underfoot drew her attention. She whipped to her right to find Iain walking down the path toward her, his hands behind his back and a sheepish smile upon his face. "There ye are, lass," he whispered huskily, as though he had been the one looking for her.

Margaret placed a hand on her hip and raised her brow. "An' there ye are." She failed to keep the bite from her voice.

Iain grimaced as he moved closer. "I am sorry I am so late. I got caught up on a project." He brought one large hand from behind his back to reveal the tiniest set of moccasins Margaret had ever laid eyes upon.

Gasping, she reached out and gingerly picked one up. She turned it this way and that in the moonlight, admiring her husband's expert leatherwork. The miniature shoes even boasted the cutest little fringe around the tops. Did this mean he still planned for them to move back home?

Her ire forgotten and new thoughts filling her mind, Margaret took both shoes into her possession before looping her arm through Iain's. "Come on in. There is rabbit stew."

"Mmm."

Iain walked with her into the cabin, where he washed up while she settled the moccasins on the table and dished up the stew. Then they bowed their heads for grace before dipping into the meal. Margaret sipped her first spoonful of stew and winced. She should not have allowed the fire to die down. But even as her hunger won out and she ate the cold stew, she could not take her eyes off the tiny shoes. Nor could she rid her mind of what they might mean. Certainly, no child within the fort wore moccasins. Though neither did the women, but Margaret continued proudly wearing hers.

Hurriedly, she downed the meal and turned to her husband. After all, this was a subject she had been eager to talk over with him since learning about her pregnancy the week before. Though Iain still had stew left in his bowl and would likely want more, he lifted a brow in question.

Margaret shook her head. "Finish eatin'," she urged. She

plucked the baby shoes from the table and turned them over in her hands once more. It made her insides dance with joy to consider how tiny and wondrous their child would be when it entered the world.

"Margaret." Iain settled his spoon in his bowl and placed a hand on her arm. "What is on yer mind?"

She met his soft, sky-blue gaze. "Are we still movin' back home? *Should* we?"

A relieved breath whooshed out of her husband's lungs. "I have been wonderin' the same thing."

Margaret sighed as her mouth tipped up at the corners, the tension fading from her shoulders. She and her husband were on the same page. Though, how silly had it been that they had each kept their concerns under wraps, rather than simply speaking with the other?

Iain sat back in his chair. "So how are ye feelin' on the matter now that we are expectin' a wee bairn?"

Margaret's smile broadened. Though one could tell that she and Iain shared a common heritage by listening to them speak, it brought her joy that they would use the same expressions she had grown up with when speaking with their child. But she sobered as she stroked her stomach. How to express what was on her mind? "I really dinnae know, Iain. I still long to return home, to share that place with this child. But I feel selfish for wantin' such a thing when the bairn could be safe here."

"I feel the same."

Her gaze snapped up to Iain's face. "Ye do?"

He nodded before he leaned forward and took her hand in his, his thumb rubbing over the back side. "I share yer feelings about livin' in the fort. I feel restless an' confined here. Even with a bounty of food on the table, life feels...limited. But, just as ye said, I feel selfish for wantin' anythin' different. When I think of that little life inside ye, I dinnae want to consider anythin' happenin' to it."

Margaret released a sigh. Her husband perfectly understood her feelings about the situation. But where did that leave them? "But then, what do we do?" She glanced up at Iain's strong, reassuring profile. Did they really have to choose between safety and happiness?

Iain rested his forehead against hers. "Margaret, I told ye before, I would follow ye to the ends of the earth. Where yer at is where I am happy. As long as we have one another an' the good Lord above, we have all we need to find happiness."

Margaret frowned. Did that mean she should be happy where she was at? After all, the Lord had blessed them endlessly. Not only did she have the Holy Spirit within her, but she had the love of her husband and her sister, as well as the precious life growing inside. And not a one of them were hungry or in danger. Then why did she feel a burning desire to return home?

Iain chuckled as he pulled back and brushed the side of her face with the back of his fingers, sending pleasant tingles across her skin. "Ye dinnae have to decide tonight. Maybe we should pray about it?"

Margaret took a deep breath and nodded. That was exactly what they needed to do. With the Lord's guidance, she might finally know their next step. And feel a peace about it.

~

Lord, please give me strength. Margaret took a deep breath of air that hinted at the coming autumn before she stepped in front of Petunia Allen's cabin. As she mounted the steps, her heart thundered against her ribcage. She lifted a hand to knock on the doorframe, but a voice stopped her before her knuckles even touched the wood.

"Come on in, Margaret," Petunia called.

"Oh, there ye are." Muireall dropped her sewing project in

the basket beside her as Margaret entered the cabin, which was lit only by the sun streaming inside the open door. When her sister stood and opened her arms for an embrace, she returned the hug hesitantly. Guilt squeezed at her throat, nearly choking her. Meanwhile, Muireall kept talking. "I knew ye were overdue for a visit. I was about to come check on ye as soon as I finished alterin' this dress for Lacy Simpson's eldest."

Margaret offered a wan smile. Her sister had not paid her a visit since she moved in with Petunia, and she doubted she would have visited today. It simply was not how things were. Muireall was always busy with her sewing, and Margaret was the one to visit. Though it did not make the conversation she needed to have with her sister any easier.

Muireall bustled back over to her rocking chair, her petticoats billowing as she went. Meanwhile, Margaret pulled over a chair from the kitchen table. Petunia kept rocking and sewing, only lifting her gaze long enough to look from Margaret to Muireall. And yet, as Petunia glanced back down with the hint of a smile on her face, 'twas as if the woman already knew what Margaret was there to discuss. Heat seared up the back of her neck.

Muireall, on the other hand, was completely oblivious. She flashed a conspiratorial grin in Margaret's direction. "I started on a surprise for the bairn today."

More heat flooded her cheeks. Would her sister even have a chance to gift the item before they left? Would she still want to? "I am sure it will be wonderful."

"Of course, it will. Now, ye will be needin' a cradle as well. Has Iain begun on one?"

Margaret's insides clenched, and though she had rarely felt ill with her pregnancy, she thought she might lose her meal. "Well, that is actually what I wanted to discuss with ye. Iain an' I are not goin' to be stayin' here."

Muireall paused, then resumed her rocking once more.

"Oh. Are ye movin' into a home outside of the fort? Is Iain goin' to build a cabin for yer growin' family?"

"No. I mean, we are movin' back home."

Muireall froze, her dark eyes turning stormy. "Home?"

"Aye. Back to the cabin."

"Why would ye want to do that? Why did we come here, then?" Her voice rose as anger laced in.

"Because I promised Ma I would make sure ye did not die in the wilderness as she and Pa did. I did it to keep ye safe. An' ye have flourished here. Look at ye." Margaret flung her hand out. "Ye are always sewin' or mendin' somethin' for someone. But it is not the same for me. I feel cramped an' confined."

Muireall shot to her feet. "So yer just goin' to deliver me here, then leave me alone to fend for meself? An' leave before I can meet me niece or nephew?" She spat the accusation at Margaret, who had to close her eyes. Her sister's words hurt because they were true. What right did she have to take away the only family Muireall had left? Tears stung her eyes.

But Iain's words came back to her, about living her life for herself, not in a cage to please her sister. Not when the Lord was calling her to go elsewhere. She did not understand the rhyme or reason to it, but she knew what she felt deep within her soul. Nights of praying had not rid her of the pull on her heart, and neither would her sister's outburst. Though, it might make it more painful.

"Muireall, this is not about ye. It is about me an' Iain, an' us livin' our lives where the Lord calls us to."

"Where the Lord calls ye? So what was it when He called ye to bring me here? Or was that only yer own will? Or what about when ye married Iain? I think ye do whatever ye very well please."

Margaret left her chair, her fists clenched at her sides as her cheeks flamed. "If I did whatever I please, we would not be here at all. If it were not for me promise to Ma, I never would have left home to begin with!"

She had not meant to yell the words, but once she had, it was as though a great weight had been lifted from her shoulders. A silence fell over the cabin as Muireall gaped at her. But for Margaret, all was suddenly clear. The Lord had used their time at the fort for good, with Muireall finding her place, but He had never meant for Margaret to stay. Her home had always been back at the cabin her father had built with his own two hands.

"Then leave," Muireall finally said with a sneer, as her tears fell.

Margaret stared at her, her heart aching. She did not wish to part like this. She longed to make things right between her and her sister before she left. But, Lord willing, there would still be time.

Suddenly, a wrinkled hand settled on Margaret's arm. Petunia gave her an almost imperceptible nod. And in that moment, she knew it was time to take her leave, that there was nothing else she could do to ease Muireall's pain at the moment. So, with one last glance at her sister, she turned and padded down the steps, out into the cool afternoon air.

As she drew in deep breaths, her own tears began to fall down her cheeks.

Lord, please. I cannae lose me sister over this.

~

*I*ain blinked as he attempted to focus on putting the last stitches on the fringed leather coat he was making for himself. Dark had long since fallen, and he worked by lamplight, straddling a bench in the vacant schoolroom that doubled as a chapel. His eyesight blurred as sleep attempted to claim him. But he needed to stay awake, needed to finish. At least, that was what he kept telling himself. It was easier that way.

Despite the promise he had made to himself, since learning about Margaret's pregnancy, he had spent extra hours tanning hides and working leather in addition to those he spent contributing his skills to the members of the fort. Iain found it much easier to focus on their journey back into the wilderness than his burgeoning bride and the implications that came with her condition. Yes, he wholeheartedly believed the child was a blessing, but fear still wound through his middle every time he considered becoming a father. Yet, when he pictured their journey home, the fears subsided and joy took their place.

So, despite the fact that his wife could use his support at the moment, Iain focused on what he knew he could do right. And at that very moment, it was tying off the thread he had used to sew the fringed leather coat. Then he gathered it and the fur-lined cloak he had made for Margaret and headed home. A yawn passed his lips as he stepped out into the dark night.

He hurried to the cabin, but when he pushed the door open, he was met with more darkness. After lighting a candle, he found a note and a plate waiting for him. *Needed Rest—Margaret* was all that was written. Iain's shoulders slumped, and he felt as though he had been punched in the stomach as he looked over at his sleeping wife, curled up facing the wall. How had he become so callous?

Laying the garments over the back of one of the straight-back chairs, he blew out the candle. Then he removed his boots and pants and slid into bed next to Margaret. Iain reached up to stroke the long, brunette tresses that escaped from her loose braid. Her shoulder rose and fell with each of her gentle breaths, and his middle squeezed tight with guilt.

Flipping over, he stared into the vast void of darkness above him. His wife deserved so much more than what he had been giving lately. While he had deluded himself into believing he was helping by preparing for their journey, it did nothing to relieve her burden as her body worked to bring new life into the world.

Iain sighed and covered his eyes as a headache attempted to creep in. The next day, he would focus solely on Margaret and her needs. He would do everything in his power to make her feel the love and support she so desperately needed. He could not let his marriage fall apart already.

CHAPTER 12

Iain set the tantalizing plates of bacon and eggs on the table before he moved to the bed and perched on the edge. Though his stomach rumbled at the smell of such a delicious meal first thing in the morning, the effort had been for his wife, not for himself. He brushed the hair from her face and gently shook her shoulder. "Margaret," he whispered.

When her forehead wrinkled in confusion, he rubbed her shoulder until her eyes blinked open under a puckered brow. "Iain?" She glanced around as though to gain her bearings. "How long did I sleep?"

"It is not too late. I woke early," he reassured her.

Margaret rose to a sitting position, her hair falling from a braid that was all a mess. Following the aroma of food, she peered at the corner table. "Ye made the meal?" Hope worked its way into her question, and she turned her gaze to him.

"Aye, darlin'." He leaned in and pressed a kiss to her forehead before moving to the table, allowing her room to rise from the bed.

In the white nightgown Petunia had made her after learning about her pregnancy, she sat on the bed and re-braided her hair before she shuffled over to the table. Stifling a yawn, she lowered herself into the seat nearest the fireplace. It had become her side, while the other had become Iain's. Margaret closed her eyes and inhaled deeply before she lifted her fork.

"Smells wonderful." Then, as soon as Iain had said a quick grace, she dived in, shoveling a heaping forkful of egg into her mouth.

Iain chuckled and followed suit.

About halfway through the meal, Margaret glanced up at him, her brow lowering again. "Is all well?"

Iain gave her a soft look. "Aye. I only realized how absent I have been an' thought I would spend the day with me beautiful bride."

Margaret actually rolled her eyes, though her lips tipped up in a grin. He chuckled again. This was the spirit that had made him fall for his wife. And the spirit he had missed by spending so much time away from her. "I believe it has been a while since I was yer bride. Do ye not have any tasks that need to be done today?"

"Nay. I completed several yesterday. In fact, I have a couple of surprises for ye when ye finish eatin'."

Margaret raised her brows, then turned back to her food, quickly shoveling the remains of her meal into her mouth. Then she pushed her plate away and turned to him expectantly.

Iain shook his head as the corners of his mouth quirked up. He stuffed the last of his bacon in his mouth and moved across the room to retrieve the garments from the end of the bed. First, he shrugged on his coat and stood before his wife.

"'Tis not quite that cold yet, is it?" She giggled, but the gleam in her eye held approval.

"I wanted us to be ready for cooler weather before we begin our journey."

Margaret stood and sauntered over, taking his lapels in her hands. "Well, ye do look mighty handsome." She leaned up and pressed a kiss to the underside of his chin.

He closed his eyes, wishing he could take her into his arms. But he had one more surprise for her. "An' this one is for ye." He lifted the cloak and wrapped it about her shoulders.

Margaret held out her arms, holding up the fur-lined hide to inspect it. "Oh, Iain, 'tis beautiful. An' warm." Though the cabin was not cool, she snuggled inside. Then she looked up at him, her gaze soft and caring. "Is this what ye have been spendin' all yer time on?"

He nodded. "A great deal of it."

She nestled into him. "These are such thoughtful gifts. Ye have put so much time an' thought into our journey an' preparin' our family."

The reverence in her voice made him stiffen, because he knew the truth. He had been avoiding her. Avoiding their child. Proving already that he was no good as a father. Though his jaw clenched, he held his wife close.

Finally, she looked up at him, and when she spoke, her voice was tentative. "Are we still leavin' in two days' time?"

Understanding that she needed his reassurance, Iain drew Margaret closer. After Muireall's outburst, they had agreed to wait a week to allow her to cool down before they made the journey back to Margaret's home. However, almost the full week had passed, and Muireall showed no signs of coming around. In fact, she had not spoken a word to Margaret. And Margaret had yet to begin preparing for their journey.

"We dinnae have to." Though he would much rather be on their way as soon as possible. He was more than ready to be free of the fort, focusing ahead, on their future. But he would do what worked best for his wife. Leaving on poor terms with her sister could not be easy. "Do ye want to try an' speak with her today?"

Margaret nodded against his chest.

"Then we will go see her directly."

With a smile, his wife rose on her tiptoes and gave him a quick kiss.

While she washed and changed, Iain took care of the dishes. And in no time, they were walking down the path to Petunia Allen's cabin. Margaret gripped his arm tightly, revealing her nerves. After walking up the steps, she knocked quietly on the door.

Muffled voices could be heard inside before the door opened only wide enough to reveal Petunia's wrinkled, leathery face. Her dark eyes shone with both seriousness and compassion. "She does not wish to see ye today."

Beside Iain, Margaret stiffened. He waited for her to say something, but the silence stretched. He spoke up. "Tell her we will leave in one week. No more. No less."

His wife's gaze snapped up to him, but Petunia gave a small nod before pushing the door to. As they turned and started their way back to their own cabin, Margaret walked stiffly ahead of him, her chin high. She would hold it together until safely indoors rather than let the other town members see her cry.

But when they entered the cabin, she whirled on him. "How dare ye do that?" She flung an arm in the direction they had just come.

"What do ye mean?"

"How dare ye issue an ultimatum like that? What if she does not come around? I cannae leave here knowin' I have ruined me relationship with me sister."

"Margaret, ye have not ruined anythin'. She has. An' if she does not come around, that is her fault, not yers. Maybe, if she knows yer actually leavin', she will think again."

Tears welled in her eyes and spilled out onto her cheeks. "But what if she does not?"

"Margaret, ye cannae live on *what ifs*. An' ye cannae live yer life for yer sister. We cannae wait forever to make this move. The weather will turn."

His wife shook her head and crossed her arms. She turned her head to face the wall, refusing to even look at him. Maybe it was the Blair blood that run through both Muireall and Margaret that made them so stubborn. "Ye dinnae understand."

Iain sighed and took a step forward. He wanted to take Margaret into his arms, to ease her pain. But somehow, in trying to help, in setting an end to this conflict between the sisters, he had made things worse. One more addition to his list of failures and shortcomings. With a sigh, he turned and left his wife alone.

~

The moment Iain stepped outside the door, Margaret's tears fell in waves as great sobs wracked her body. She took solace curled on the bed as rain pattered on the roof, mirroring the sorrow that consumed her. How was she following God's path if she was losing everyone who meant anything to her in the process? This could not be God's plan. And yet, it was her reality. After nearly a week, her sister still refused to see her, much less speak with her. And now her husband had walked out as well.

"God, what do I do?"

If she agreed to move in a week, regardless of where matters stood with Muireall, she might regain her husband's favor. But she might lose Muireall in the process. But if she did not agree to leave in a week, did not agree to leave before Muireall came around, would it drive an irreparable wedge between she and her husband? The thought of causing such damage to their relationship, when Iain already seemed distant so often these days, broke her heart as thoroughly as the thought of losing her tie with her sister.

Iain was the first person, besides maybe her father, who had ever accepted her so completely as she was. His love for her was a balm to her soul that she had not realized she needed. Especially once they were back home in the wilderness, alone, how would she cope without that comfort? Why did there have to be a choice at all?

Margaret's sobs came with new strength.

Iain knocked on the door of James Harrod's cabin. Who knew why he had come here instead of retreating to the quiet chapel where he normally did his leatherwork? But it was where his feet had brought him. Maybe he was hoping for advice from a man who had been married for several years and already had a son. Either way, he waited before the large cabin at the corner of the fort and knocked a second time.

The door swung open after a moment, and Harrod's smiling face greeted him. "Donegal! Come on in out of the rain." He motioned Iain in and led him over to where several other men already sat around a table twice the size of the one in his and Margaret's cabin.

"I was just telling the men that I suppose we will have to postpone the hunt tomorrow if this weather does not break." Harrod settled into his chair.

Iain nodded, taking his own seat, though his mind was far from hunting and weather. In fact, the lull of the rain on the roof simply pulled him deeper into the old, familiar pit of despair.

"Meh. It will stop before sunrise. You watch and see." Lester Clapton pointed a scrawny finger in their direction as he ran his tongue over rotting teeth. Several other men harrumphed as though they disagreed.

"'Twill believe it when I see it," the broad, red-headed Angus Cameron countered. "Me wife will be glad to have me home to boss around, anyway." He chuckled, but from previous encounters, Iain could tell the man loved his wife whole-heartedly. And they had a whole passel of children with the same red hair.

"True. My wife has been asking me to build a cradle before the baby comes." Andrew Saxton was a young man, barely twenty, with bright blond hair and green eyes.

Harrod chuckled. "Is your wife not due any day now?"

Saxton grimaced before he stood. "Yes. I guess I should get on that. Nice talking, gentlemen." He gave a nod before he took his leave.

"Yer expectin' a bairn, too, are ye not?" Cameron turned his brown gaze upon Iain, and every eye at the table did the same.

"Aye," Iain replied tightly, without elaborating.

Harrod's brows lowered. "What is on your mind? All is well with the babe, I hope."

Iain glanced at him. Had Harrod read his thoughts? He could not share his marital problems before all these men, but he could share the bit that Harrod would need to know. "Margaret an' I have decided to move back to her family's homestead, farther south."

Harrod gave a slow nod. "Well, we hate to see you go, but we know that fort life does not suit everyone. When do you plan to leave?"

Iain twisted his mouth to the side as he poked at a crack in the wood of the table. "Well, we have not yet decided. Her sister will be stayin' here, an' she has not taken the news well."

"Ah. And Margaret does not wish to part on poor terms."

"Aye." Iain blew out a breath, the man having read his mind once again.

"Ain't that just like a woman," Lester interjected, earning a glare from nearly everyone at the table. Best Iain could remember, the man was single and always had been.

"Is yer wife not worth the wait?" Cameron's question was direct and difficult. How could Iain explain without revealing his past? He struggled for the right words.

"Of course, she is. But I cannae be a good husband to her here. I am afraid our marriage will fall apart before we are able to leave."

Harrod cocked his head, his fingers steepled together over the table. "What makes you a bad husband here?"

Iain worked his jaw, his teeth pressing tightly together. He could not explain his past to this man. He might get thrown out on the spot.

Harrod leaned forward. "Iain, I am not sure there is a right or wrong answer here. I think you will regret it if you do not give your wife the time she needs. And I think she will regret it if she follows her sister's whims instead of stepping into the life you have made and agreed upon. But you do have to be in agreeance, no matter what. Otherwise, there will be pain and resentment, on both parts."

Iain groaned when Cameron nodded his agreement. These men had a fair point. Though Margaret was being unreasonable, he could not push her.

"Oh, come on. All he needs is a good, stiff drink." Clapton pulled a flask from his pocket and plunked it on the table before Iain.

At the sight of it, Iain's heart nearly stopped, and the breath stalled within his lungs. Even after all the years, he could imagine exactly how deliciously cold the metal would be to his touch and what the drink would feel like as it slid down his throat. The warm burning would start in his middle with an accompanying haze.

But then would follow the hurt and pain that had once

plagued him, as well as a deep, horrible self-loathing. No, he could never go back there again.

"What is the matter? You look like you seen a ghost."

He glanced up at the man. But in his memory, he could see only the faces of those two boys as they peered out the window while he beat their father. Without a word, he pushed away from the table and stood. "I am sorry to take yer time, men, but I need to get back to me wife."

Replies came as he departed from the room, but none of them registered. All he could think of was getting as far away from that drink as possible. Soft rain once again falling on his skin, he marched along the muddied path to their cabin. Then he clopped up the steps and into the room.

Margaret's eyes widened as she looked up from the fire where she was cooking. "Iain, are ye all right?"

"We leave tomorrow."

Her mouth dropped open as she stood. "Tomorrow? Iain, what happened to one week? We cannae even be packed in a day."

Though he doubted her last words were true, he faltered. He needed his wife in this or all would be for naught. "Then in three days' time."

"Three days. Iain, what has happened?" Her face was stricken, as though she did not truly wish to know the answer.

And he was not sure he could give one. For, if he told his wife the truth, would she even still want him as a husband and father? As he stared at her large, questioning eyes, his heart felt as though it might beat of out of his chest. Emotions circled his throat and threatened to clog it off. He turned to leave, but Margaret's voice, laced with tears, stopped him.

"Iain. Iain, please dinnae leave. Please talk to me. Please tell me what ye have done."

He closed his eyes as the truth washed over him. Margaret's first thought was that it was his fault, that they were fleeing because of some wrong he had committed. Maybe that was the answer he had needed. There was no place for him at the fort and apparently, no place for him with his own wife.

His words came out tight and hollow. "I will leave in three days' time. Ye can come with me or ye can stay." Then he walked out.

~

Margaret slowly pulled herself from the world of sleep. Her head ached and felt as though it had been stuffed full of cotton. Rubbing her hands over her face revealed that it was still as puffy as it felt. But that was what happened when one cried themselves to sleep.

Her body still heavy with sorrow, the pain in her heart was torn open once again when she glanced around the room. Iain had not come home the night before. But where could he have gone? Where had he been the day before when he came back in such a rush to leave? What was happening with her husband that he could not share with her?

With a groan, Margaret forced herself from the bed and over to the washbasin atop the hutch where she splashed water on her face. Her stomach had begun to bloom recently and today, the burden weighed heavily on her. Moving to the edge of the bed, she unbraided her hair to brush it.

How little she knew about her husband and his past. However, she did know the character he had shown her in the few months she had known him, and it spoke volumes about the man he was. This new version that had stormed out on her twice in one day did not align with that.

But how could she help if he shut her out? And more importantly, did she even still have a marriage to save?

A new sob tried to tear from Margaret's throat, but she forced it back down. There was no point in shedding more tears. It would do her no good. It would not bring her sister's favor on her move, and it would not heal the rift between her and her husband. Plus, it only made her feel worse, as though her limbs were made of lead.

Instead, she lifted herself from the bed and went to the pantry, where she withdrew a strip of jerked meat. Settling at the table, she forced the food past her lips. Even if she did not feel like consuming anything, her bairn would need the nourishment.

No matter how difficult it was, she had a decision to make. And yet, how could she choose between her husband and her sister when it seemed they had both cast her aside, just as her mother had done all her life? Thrown her aside in favor of her sister. Even as her mother had laid dying, she had asked Margaret to forget herself and save her sister—save her sister from the same fate as her parents. Margaret had done that, done as her mother asked. And what good had come of it?

Her sister would not speak with her, her husband might leave her, and at the moment, she was left questioning if either of them actually loved her. For if they did, would her wants and needs not matter? Hopelessness and loneliness threatened to rise up and swallow her whole, but to combat it, Margaret took to the outdoors. Grabbing up her basket, she headed for the gardens.

Outside her cabin was a beautiful fall day. The warm sun was cloaked by a welcoming breeze, while the very first yellow leaves peeked from behind the greens. But the perfection of the day could not seem to push away the gloom that had taken root within her soul.

As she walked down the path, a motion ahead caught her attention. A hunched figured headed toward her. Narrowing her gaze, she recognized the person to be Petunia. Her brows came together. Never had Margaret seen the woman outside her home. And yet, here she was, shuffling toward Margaret with determination in her tiny steps.

Margaret lengthened her own stride to meet the woman. "Petunia, what brings ye out today?"

The woman's dark eyes were piercing as she lifted her gaze to Margaret's face, her mouth drawn. "'Tis yer sister. She has taken ill."

Cold washed over Margaret. "What do ye mean?"

"It is the ague. She has taken to the bed, an' I cannae wake her."

"Nay." Margaret breathed the word.

Petunia did not utter another sound but turned and started her determined shuffle in the other direction. Margaret fought her feet to keep them from running past the woman, to her sister. Instead, she stayed dutifully and respectfully at Petunia's side. She had never realized quite how bent the woman's short frame was until she stood beside her. Petunia did not even come to her shoulder. Unlike her sewing, her movements were tight and rigid. And yet, she covered the distance quicker than Margaret would have thought possible.

When they reached the cabin, she could not contain herself any longer. After dashing up the steps, she threw open the door and went to the bedside. Dropping her basket on the floor, she leaned over and put the back of her hand to Muireall's sweat-dampened forehead. Her skin was flaming hot. Quiet wheezes came with each labored breath.

"Oh, Muireall," Margaret cried. "Ye cannae do this to me. I willna let ye leave me like this."

CHAPTER 13

argaret jerked at the sudden touch of a hand on her shoulder.

"Ye need to eat, Margaret, dearie." Petunia held out a bowl of broth.

Blinking, Margaret lifted her head and looked up at Muireall, whose skin was still as pale as ever and glistening with sweat. She must have fallen asleep keeping watch. She rose, went to the head of the bed, and re-wetted the rag on Muireall's forehead. Then, silently, she accepted the bowl of nourishment from Petunia.

The woman placed a wrinkled hand on her arm. "I will try to get some of the broth in her."

Margaret nodded but did not meet Petunia's gaze. She was too numb. Not only was her sister on the brink of death, she had been unable to get word to Iain of her sister's condition. She had allowed herself two quick trips back to their cabin, but each time, she had found it devoid of her husband. And he had not come looking for her on his own. She moved to the table and simply focused on consuming one spoonful of broth at a time. And when, at last, the bowl was empty, she returned to her sister's bedside.

Petunia stood on a small wooden stool in order to reach her sister's head as she attempted to the coax broth past her lips. But though some went into her mouth, there was no movement at her throat to indicate that she had swallowed. Still, they must do all they could.

"Here, let me try, an' ye can prepare her some of that tea."

Petunia handed over the bowl and shuffled past her to the stone fireplace to heat a kettle of water.

Margaret slipped her hand behind her sister's head, into her damp, raven-black hair, to tip it forward and urge her to drink. But it was no use. Muireall was far from them, lost to a world of sleep and sickness. After a few more failed attempts, Margaret withdrew her sweat-soaked hand and focused instead on re-wetting the fabric covering her forehead. It seemed it took no time at all before the cloth was heated through.

When Petunia returned with a cup of tea, Margaret traded her the bowl of broth. Then she resumed her efforts to coax Muireall to drink. Though it seemed an impossible task, each drop that passed her sister's mouth could be lifesaving. While Margaret did not know what plants or herbs were in the tea Petunia had prepared time and time again over the past day and night, she trusted in the woman's knowledge and prayed that it healed whatever ailed her sister.

It seemed that was all she had done since arriving was pray. Constantly. And yet, Muireall's condition remained stagnant. Still, when nothing else could be done, Petunia came to perch at the end of the bed, and they both prayed. And when Margaret could not find the words to pray on her own, she took solace in Petunia's aged voice as she called out to the Lord. "Dear Heavenly Father, we humbly ask for Yer mercy upon this child of Yers. Please lay Yer healin' hand upon her, Lord. Please take this illness from her body."

Petunia continued on, but Margaret lost track of the words as she gripped Muireall's hand and watched her youthful face for any hint of change. Behind her, the prayer transitioned to a hymn, and she found herself humming along, though she did not know the words. She stood and re-wetted the rag before resuming her post and taking Muireall's clammy hand back into hers.

A short time after noon, Margaret jerked awake as her head fell forward. She stood to re-wet the cloth, but Petunia was already doing so. The little woman was as unflagging as a draft horse. Though Margaret had fallen asleep multiple times as she sat silently by her sister's side, she was not aware that Petunia had slept a single wink. And yet, she had kept them in constant supply of broth and tea. Heaven only knew where the woman found the energy, but Margaret was beginning to suspect there was an incredible power within her slight frame. Margaret's respect for Petunia had grown tenfold in the short time they had been tending to her sister.

As she scrubbed her hands over her face in an effort to wake herself, a quiet tapping came at the door. Margaret stopped and turned to listen, her brows pulled together as she waited to see if she had imagined the sound, for it was so faint. The knocking came again, only slightly louder than the first time. She walked over to the door and opened it wide, allowing the warm, inviting sun to stream into the dark, dismal cabin.

Betty stood beyond the doorway, an apologetic smile on her face as she held up a white-oak basket with a faded blue-plaid cloth covering its contents. "I did not wish to disturb you, but I brought bread."

For the first time since she had encountered Petunia the day before, a small smile stretched Margaret's lips. "Thank ye. Come on in." She motioned Betty inside, pulling the door to behind her.

"I do not know if it helped, but when my baby sister was ill one time when we lived in the colonies, the doctor told us the sunlight would help her. She was little, though, young enough that we could actually carry her outdoors for stretches of time while the sun was shining." She raised her broad shoulders as though to shrug off her own words. However, Margaret was desperate for any piece of information that could help. Nothing else had worked so far, and her sister was disturbingly far gone.

Margaret glanced at Petunia, who gave her a nod without her having to utter a word. Margaret walked over and re-opened the door, allowing the warmth of the sun to settle over her sister while a gentle breeze filtered into the cabin, cutting through the mustiness. Plus, the sunshine brightened Margaret's spirits a bit. For the first time since Muireall had fallen ill, the world did not seem quite so hopeless and dreary.

Margaret went to Betty, who towered over her but shifted restlessly from one foot to the other as though she was not sure if she was welcome. She took the basket and set it on the table to take Betty's hand in hers. "Thank ye for that suggestion."

A broad grin broke out across the woman's tanned face. "I am glad to help. Want me to slice the bread? I brought cheese too." Suddenly, she seemed comfortable and in her element, as though helping was what she preferred to do most.

Margaret allowed herself a sigh of relief as her stomach gurgled. "That sounds wonderful." Settling at the table, she watched Betty bustle about the cabin, serving them bread and cheese, a welcome change from the broth that had sustained them thus far. When Betty had joined her at the table and she had peeked in Muireall's direction to reassure herself there had been no change, she addressed the woman. "Thank ye for thinkin' of us."

Betty's broad smile flashed again. "'Tis no problem. We take care of our own around here. I know you do not always get along with Mary, but I believe you to be a friend. And, well, I do not have many of those. So I will do what I can for my friends when I can."

Margaret offered her a soft smile. Though the woman could be boisterous, if even a bit annoying, she was always friendly and positive. "I would be glad to be counted as a friend of yers, Betty. I must admit that I have trouble making friends as well." She frowned as regret tugged at her heart. Her gaze slid to her sister, who she had not spoken with in days

Misunderstanding the look that must have passed over Margaret's face, Betty placed her hand on Margaret's arm. "I feel deep in my heart that you will come out on the other side of this stronger. That all will be well."

Tears welled in Margaret's eyes. "More than anythin', I wish that to be true." While she could not bear the thought of losing her sister, she certainly could not bear losing her without having made amends. Her tears spilled over onto her cheeks, and she let them fall. For all the time she had spent beside her sister's bed, she had cried such few tears. Instead, there had been an overwhelming sense of numbness.

While she cried, Betty came around the table and held her. And finally, having come to the realization that she had a friend outside of her family, she wept on Betty's shoulder as a multitude of emotions washed over her. Then, when the last tear had fallen, she sat up and wiped her eyes, taking a deep breath.

Betty smiled and moved to Petunia's side. While she towered over the little woman, more than twice her size in both height and weight, she put a gentle hand on her arm and told her to let her know if she needed anything. Then she went to Muireall and whispered a prayer of healing over her, praying for both Margaret and Petunia as well. Tears welled in Margaret's eyes again.

"Thank ye," she told Betty as she headed for the door.

Betty turned back, her brown eyes warm. "I will leave you be for now, but do not hesitate to let me know if you need anything at all."

Margaret smiled and nodded. Though she appreciated the offer, she and Petunia were capable on their own. But then awareness swept through her. Iain. She hesitated. Did her husband even care anymore? But she could not ignore the nagging at her heart.

She glanced back at Petunia, then stepped outside into the sunshine with Betty. "There is one thing," she said quietly.

Betty nodded enthusiastically, wide-eyed. Then she leaned closer so that Margaret could whisper her request.

"If ye see me husband, can ye let him know where I am?"

She did not elaborate and thankfully, Betty asked no questions. Instead, she gave Margaret a warm, understanding smile. "Of course."

"Thank ye," Margaret told her friend once again before she ducked back into the cabin. And as she settled back in the chair beside her sister, her heart felt just a little lighter than it had.

~

*I*ain rubbed his fingers under Goldie's snow-white mane as guilt tugged at him for the millionth time since leaving Margaret. For two nights, he had resisted the urge to go home and see to his wife. But his hurt and fear had still been sharp and fresh, so he had joined his horse in the shelter for the farm animals. He had been unable to face Margaret and the disappointment that was written all over her face as he had made his callous decree. But the longer he was away, and the closer his three-day ultimatum drew, the more he yearned to return to his wife and make matters right between them.

But thoughts and questions swirled in his mind, rolling

over and over, unanswered. How was he to remedy the situation? Apologizing and explaining, as he should have done long ago? Could he take back his words and stand by Margaret, giving her the time that she needed when temptation was knocking on his door? He feared, more than anything, that he was not a strong enough man to resist the draw of the drink.

Iain let out a sigh and ran his hand through his hair. He had failed himself and so many others in the past, and it seemed to weigh on him like a shackle. An anchor to his past that would never let him move on. But Margaret deserved so much more. *He* desired to be more, to be better...for her.

As a cool breeze tugged at the mare's mane and gently kissed Iain's face, he realized there was only one way he could make things right and move forward. He dropped to his knees, right there in the animal corral, where all of creation could see.

"Lord, I have failed Ye. I promised that if Ye brought me back to Margaret, I would be the best husband I could. Instead, I have failed her time an' time again. I allowed all the lies of the past to worm their way back in an' ran away from me troubles instead of trustin' in Ye. Lord, I know that when I sought Ye with an honest heart, Ye saved me an' made me new. I know Ye cast the mistakes of me past into the ocean. An' yet, I have been wearin' them around as a heavy yoke. Lord, I need Yer help to truly leave the past behind me. To move forward an' make a future followin' in Yer will. Please Lord, help me to correct this situation with Margaret an' be the man she needs."

Feeling as though a weight had been lifted, Iain released a breath and straightened his shoulders. Then, he gave Goldie's neck one last pat and headed toward the cabin. And his wife. A few scattered leaves, the first to fall for autumn, crunched under his boots even though green grass still abounded. Walking up the steps to the door, he stopped to take another deep breath before he pushed it open.

Yet when he entered, his brow bunched. His wife was

nowhere in sight. He sighed and turned back toward the door. Likely, she was out in the gardens. He stepped back out into the setting afternoon sun. Would Margaret still be in the gardens this late? Considering it was her favorite place, it was worth checking. He took the worn path in front of the cabins.

At first glance, the vegetable patch seemed devoid of people. Though a cool breeze rustled through the still-green plants, no conversation drifted to his ears and no heads rose above the stalks. Frowning, he walked through, peering down the rows. What if Margaret was bent, collecting the last of the summer squash? When he had made it past one garden plot and started along the other, a head did pop up above the tops of the green plants, though the woman was much too tall for Margaret, with lighter hair.

However, when she spotted him, the woman made a beeline in his direction, as though she had meant to come see him all along. Iain waited where he was. What did the woman want? As she drew closer, he recognized Betty Davidson.

"Mr. Donegal, I was hoping to run to into you. I was visiting with your wife earlier today."

Iain's heart leapt, and he had to fight to keep the relieved joy from his voice. "Ye were?"

"Yes. At Petunia Allen's place. What with her staying at her sister's bedside during her illness, I took bread and cheese over."

It was all Iain could do not to gape at the woman who so carefully told him exactly what he needed to know without ever revealing awareness of a single thing amiss between him and his wife. Swallowing, he nodded. "Thank ye very much for that, Mrs. Davidson. I am sure that Margaret was very grateful for yer kindness. An' I am thankful to ye for bein' a good friend to her."

Betty gave him a knowing smile. "The pleasure is all mine,

sir. Your wife is a wonderful woman, and I am blessed to count her as a friend. I pray all works out well for her."

Iain could only nod as a knot lodged in his throat. Betty seemed to understand, for she took her leave to return to her gardening while he turned and set his feet in the direction of Petunia Allen's cabin.

CHAPTER 14

Margaret bent over the pot of broth as she reheated it, though her sister remained unaware of her surroundings and made no effort to eat. The hot fire crackled, setting Margaret to sweating. She used her free hand to wave at her face as she stirred.

Petunia came shuffling up, giving a small chuckle. "Ye go on an' tend to yer sister. I will finish this up."

Thankful for the swap, Margaret fled from the heat and to Muireall's side. Gladly dipping her hands in the cool water at the bedside, she re-wet the cloth from her forehead. However, as she laid the cloth down, she paused. Drying her hand on her apron, she reached back up and pressed her hand against her sister's cheek. With a gasp, she turned to Petunia. "Her fever has broken!"

She could not even be mad at the woman when she gave a small, knowing nod, the wrinkles at the sides of her mouth increased by her wry smile. Margaret let out a relieved breath as a smile tugged at her own mouth. Though Muireall had not awakened and wheezes still came with each breath she took, her sister was finally on the mend.

Margaret looked up at the ceiling. "Thank Ye, Lord," she whispered. In her heart of hearts, she knew God would bring Muireall through. She settled into the chair beside the bed and started singing a hymn, the first that came to mind.

~

When Iain approached Petunia Allen's cabin, the blessed sound of his wife's voice met his ears. For a moment, he simply stopped and listened to the joyous melody that furthered the healing in his heart the Lord had already begun. If Iain could earn Margaret's forgiveness and favor after she learned the truth of his past, then maybe they could move forward. With that thought, he mounted the steps and stood in the open doorway. His presence cast a shadow over his wife where she sat at the bedside, singing over her sister's pale, unmoving body. His insides clenched before Margaret spun around.

"Iain," she breathed.

He paused at the sight of her, of her beauty and grace. How could he have walked away from such a woman? "Can we speak?"

She hesitated, glancing at Muireall before she turned back to him. It must be difficult for her to step away with her sister in such a condition. But she nodded, then stood to follow him outside.

Back in the sunshine, Iain glanced around, searching for somewhere private. Though he needed to explain his situation and ask Margaret's forgiveness, he did not wish to air his darkest secrets for the whole world to hear. When the fort's little chapel came to mind, he led her to the one-room cabin. He chose a seat, and as Margaret settled onto the log bench next to him, he took her hands into his.

His wife looked up at him expectantly but with no animosity, despite his recent behavior. It fed the guilt coiling deep inside, but he did not let it stop him from what needed to be done. It was time his wife knew about his past. Closing his eyes, he began.

"I know there is no excuse for me behavior the last several days, but I need to explain why I have been so absent. Growin' up, me father was a drunkard who beat me mother. She was a sweet, gentle, God-fearin' woman, an' the only person in the world that loved me. Yet when she passed, I fell into the same drinkin' pattern as me father. Even with a drink in hand, I was desperate for the next. One night, I was broke, roamin' the streets. I passed a man sportin' a handsome pocket watch that would fetch a pretty penny. When I tried to rob him of it, he struggled, an' I beat the man."

Margaret sucked in a breath, her eyes wide, but listened attentively without pulling away.

So he continued. "But as I raised me fist to punch him, I looked up. I realized we were outside his home, an' his two boys were starin' out the window at the two of us, their faces stricken with fear. An' in that moment, I realized I had become me father."

Iain stopped to shake his head. "I ran away as far as I could from the pain an' temptation. That is why I was alone in the wilderness when we met. I lived as a long hunter an' guide, avoidin' connections that could lead me back there. Then, the other day, the reason I wanted to leave suddenly was because I had to face that temptation again. A man at Harrod's place had offered me his flask."

Margaret's hand flew to her mouth. "Oh, Iain."

"I did not partake, Margaret." He met her gaze. "But it terrified me. I did not wish to stay here where I could be tempted again. I did not want to risk turnin' into that man again. I did not want to do that to ye or our bairn." Though Margaret gave him a pointed look, he pressed on. "Yet when ye accused me of doin' wrong, I thought ye believed the worst of me. I thought ye thought me as terrible as I thought meself. Not only did I lash out, but I ran. An' I can never be sorry enough."

"Iain." His name was a breath on her lips before she shook her head. His gut tightened. "When ye left me like that..." Tears formed in his wife's eyes. "I thought ye did not care. That ye did not love me."

"Margaret." He swept her up into his arms and pulled her close, needing her to feel his love. "Oh, darlin', if ye will have me, I never want to make ye feel that way again."

She looked up at him, smiling through her tears. "Of course, I will have ye. I vowed to stand by ye an' love ye, for better or worse, for all our days. An' I plan to do exactly that."

He wanted to believe her words with everything in him. "Even with all I told ye?"

Margaret nodded her head before she laid a hand upon his heart. "Iain, that man is not the man I married. He is not the one I have fallen in love with all these months."

"I love ye, too, darlin'." Iain pressed a kiss to her forehead before he pulled her close again, soaking in the feel of her. Then, after several moments, he leaned back to look down into her face. "An' we will not leave until Muireall is well an' ye are ready to go. If the weather turns, then we will face that as it comes. With the Lord on our side."

Her grin widened. "Her fever broke today. Just before ye arrived."

He gave her one more hug before he set her aside and stood. "That is wonderful. Now let us get ye back to her side."

With an appreciative smile, his wife stood and nestled into his side as they made the short walk back to Petunia's cabin. As the setting sun filtered over them, Iain could not help but whisper a prayer of thanks to God for restoring his marriage. Now, if Margaret's relationship with her sister could also be mended, all would be well.

The tiny room was crowded, but joy abounded in Margaret's soul as she shoveled in another delectable bite of the hearty beef stew, she, Iain, and Petunia had prepared together that evening. Though Muireall had yet to awaken, she slept peacefully while Petunia rocked at the end of the bed. Iain and Margaret sat beside one another in straight-backed chairs alongside the bed. Rubbing a hand over her burgeoning belly, Margaret sighed.

"M-Margaret."

Her eyes widened at the tiny, hoarse whisper of her name. Muireall's eyes were barely open, and her skin was pale as ever, but she was awake. Margaret handed her bowl of stew to Iain, perched on the side of the bed, and took Muireall's hand.

Muireall's lips stretched into the beginnings of a smile. "Yer here."

"Of course I am." Tears welled in her eyes as she squeezed Muireall's hand.

"I thought..." Muireall closed her eyes and swallowed, the pain in her face evident as her brows came together.

Margaret grabbed a cup and dipped out water from the basin beside her, bringing it to Muireall's lips. Her sister took a few sips before she settled her head back on the pillow.

Margaret placed a hand on Muireall's shoulder. "Ye rest now. We can speak later."

Muireall barely dipped her chin in a nod and then was quiet as her breaths became soft and even.

Petunia came up and squeezed Margaret's arm. "All will be well now."

Margaret nodded, but she could not speak as grateful tears welled up from her throat. Aye, all would be well now. The Lord had brought them through the darkness. Turning to Iain, she walked over and settled in his lap, wrapping her arms around her husband's neck.

Just that morning, both her husband and sister had seemed lost to her. But before the sun had set, God had restored them both. She could not wait to see what He did next.

~

Iain lifted his stiff limbs from the hard floor, then stretched out the soreness. Though his body protested, he was glad for the sleeping arrangements. For he was near his wife, who slept in a bed with her sister while Petunia slumped in her favorite rocker. He stood, and his wife smiled up at him. Before he could protest, she had swung her legs from the bed and come to meet him, a smile on her lips. He wrapped his arms around her expanding waist and dropped a kiss on her mouth as she brought her face up to his.

"Good mornin'." She grinned.

"Good mornin'." He rumbled his response before he bent and kissed her cheek as well.

Then, to his surprise, a third "good mornin'" croaked from the bed. Margaret gasped and turned toward her sister, who had slept soundly through the night after her brief waking the previous day. He followed his wife to the head of the bed. Iain prayed that when Muireall was finally strong enough to talk, the two would make amends.

"How are ye feelin'?"

"Thirsty."

Margaret dipped water and helped her sister drink. Then, miraculously, Muireall pushed up in bed. She breathed heavily as though it took a great effort, and Margaret put a hand to her shoulder.

"Slow down. Ye dinnae need to overdo it."

Muireall gave her a small smile. "I feel much better. An' I

need to speak with ye." When her tone turned serious, Iain looked at his wife, and his stomach clenched. Margaret's mouth pressed into a line, but she nodded. Muireall reached out and took her hand, tears forming in her eyes before she even started to speak.

"I am so sorry, Margaret, for how I have acted. It was wrong of me to want ye to stay here on me behalf. I cannae imagine me life without ye, but I cannae hold ye back. Ye have a life with Iain now." Muireall offered him a tiny smile.

"We never meant to hurt ye," Margaret returned. "This has been heavy on our hearts, Muireall. The decision was not easy. An' I had not found the strength to leave without yer blessin', but it is what we feel the Lord is callin' us to do."

Muireall nodded. "Ye have me blessin' now, Margaret." Tears shone in her eyes, and though her voice came out strained, she still smiled.

Iain could not help the pride and joy that surged through his chest. Not only for the maturity his sister-in-law had achieved through her ordeal, but for the blessing of their journey. With him, Margaret, and Muireall together and at ease with one another, compared to where they had been two days before, he could not deny—the Lord truly worked all for His good. Even the bad.

~

"Careful," Margaret advised as Muireall stepped down onto the first step, exiting Petunia's cabin, though she held her sister's hand as well as kept an arm around her shoulder.

Muireall gave her a pointed look, a healthy gleam in her dark blue eyes. "I am not made of glass."

Margaret could barely suppress her smile as they continued their descent. "Aye. But ye are on the mend."

Though her sister was regaining her strength quickly, it had only been two days since Muireall had awakened and they had made amends. Her heart clenched. Would she truly be ready to leave in a week, as she and Iain had discussed earlier that morning? If the cool breeze that ruffled their hair and the autumn scent in the air were any indication, they could not wait too long.

Margaret hugged her arm tighter around her sister as they left the path to meander the gardens. "I told Iain we would try an' leave in a week, as long as the weather cooperates."

Muireall nodded, then gave her a serious look. "Ye be careful."

She returned her sister's nod, her free hand going to her belly. Though excitement coursed through her each time she considered going home, so did worry. The trip had been arduous enough the first time, with Iain nearly losing his life. But now, she would be making the journey four months pregnant. "I will be," she finally reassured Muireall.

"Good." Her sister blinked back tears. As they passed by the resilient tomato plants that continued to produce, Betty rose from her squatted position, her bright smile greeting them.

"Oh, what a wonderful surprise." Dropping her basket, she scurried over and embraced them both in a hug. "I told Margaret all would be well," she said to Muireall when she relinquished them from her grip.

Muireall grinned at her. "Thank ye for all that ye did. It really means a lot that ye helped Margaret and Petunia through. If ye ever need anythin', please let us know. An' come visit. Me an' Petunia get lonely sometimes, just a sittin' there sewin'."

Betty beamed at Muireall. "Absolutely." Then she turned to Margaret, her smile dimming. "I hear you are leaving us."

Margaret sighed, her heart aching at the other woman's

sorrow. "We are. But I will miss ye dearly." She prayed Betty understood how sincere she was.

But the taller woman remained stoic. Though tears formed in her eyes, she smiled and put a hand on Muireall's arm. "I will keep an eye on this one for you. Make sure she keeps her strength up and gets some fresh air every now and then."

"That would be perfect." Margaret fought back tears as she smiled.

Betty dismissed herself, returning to the tomatoes so they could resume their walk, which thankfully, kept Margaret from crying in front of the other two. There would be nothing easy about leaving behind those she held dear, but to see them all growing so close helped ease her mind. She could count on Petunia, Muireall, and Betty to take care of one another. And with the transformation her sister had gone through since her brush with death, she would truly begin to flourish.

As she steered Muireall back toward the cabins, she could once again find joy in the journey that lay before her and Iain. Her insides fluttered with excitement as she turned her face to the warm sun.

CHAPTER 15

"*I* hope the rain stops afore tomorrow." Margaret frowned as she finished folding her orange dress and glanced toward Iain, who sat cleaning his rifle at the table. Rain pattered on the roof, falling steadily as it had all day long.

"I am sure it will." He stopped and turned his sky-blue gaze upon her, giving her a gentle smile. "But if it does not, we will stay another day." His nonchalance about when they left eased her anxieties.

Margaret returned his smile before she resumed her packing.

Angus Cameron had stopped by the day before to bring a wooden rattle he had made for the baby, as well as a packet of tomato seeds his wife had prepared for them. Margaret had teared up as the broad man had clapped Iain on his shoulder and told him he would be a wonderful father.

Margaret slid her stack of folded clothes next to the rattle and baby moccasins on the bed. Before she could retrieve her mother's Bible from the mantel, a hurried knocking came at the door. Margaret grinned.

After Angus's visit the day before, there had been a nearly

constant stream of visitors today, wishing them well and bearing gifts. Due to the generosity of the townsfolk, Goldie would be heavily laden on their return trip. The outpouring of love did warm her heart, even if she had not felt it in the days before. Another such visitor must be at the door now.

Margaret hurried over and swung the door open as the knocking started up again. But when she did, Petunia, Muireall, and Betty all came streaming into the cabin, their arms laden with gifts. Margaret gasped, her hands going to her mouth. As she shut the door, Iain propped his rifle against the wall and stood to greet their guests, who quickly filled their table with pots of food and presents wrapped in fabric. Both sweet cinnamon and hearty spice drifted to Margaret's nose.

"What is all of this?" Margaret smiled as she looked around at all the faces.

Muireall grinned. "We didna want ye to have to cook on yer last night here."

"And we brought gifts for the baby...or *bairn*." Betty giggled at her use of their Scottish term.

Margaret shook her head as tears sprang to her eyes. "Oh, this is too much. Ye should not have gone to all this trouble."

Petunia's tan, wrinkled face creased further into a hearty smile. "'Twas no trouble at all."

Margaret hugged each of the women in turn before she moved to the table. She lifted a brow as she glanced at her friends. "Gifts or food first?"

"Gifts," both Muireall and Betty cheered.

Laughing, Margaret settled at the table and pulled the smallest package toward her. Untying and removing the fabric wrapping, she revealed several pouches of herbs, as well as a leather journal filled with recipes in slanted handwriting. She turned to Petunia, knowing exactly who it was from.

The old woman waved a hand as if to dismiss whatever she was about to say. "Now, dinnae go gettin' emotional on me. Just an old lady helpin' pass down the knowledge to the younger folk." Still, Margaret went to Petunia and gave her a heartfelt embrace.

Returning to her seat, she pulled the largest package over. When she removed the fabric wrapped around it, it revealed a pieced-together baby quilt that had to have been made by Betty's hand. Much like the owner, it was quirky and unique, while beautiful to its core. The squares were every color imaginable, though often not squares at all, that came together to form a stunning rainbow that would brighten her baby's life. Tears filled her eyes as she held it open to enjoy every inch of its beauty, then brought it close to her heart. "Thank ye," she whispered before she went to the tall woman and hugged her. Betty gave a long, tight squeeze filled with sniffles.

"All right, mine last." Muireall stood with a smile on her lips and hands behind her back as she waited for Margaret to open the gift.

She unwrapped the fabric to lay eyes upon the gown her sister had been completing for the baby. The white gown with white leaves and flowers embroidered around the collar was simply perfection. Every stitch showed her sister's expert craftmanship as well as her love for the child.

"It is absolutely beautiful, Muireall."

Her sister grinned but nodded her head toward the package. "That is not all."

Brows drawn together, Margaret laid the gown aside to stare down at an intricate masterpiece. Lifting it and allowing it to open up, she found Proverbs 31 embroidered in an exquisite, flower-and-greenery-filled frame. Every inch, every word, was hand stitched. But the longer she looked, the more familiar some of the colors and patterns seemed. She turned to Muireall. "Is this...?"

Muireall nodded. "It is what I have been workin' on since

Ma passed. I started it because I missed her so much. But now that yer goin' to be a mither, I think ye should have it."

Tears welled again as she shook her head. "I cannae."

"Ye can, an' ye will." Muireall gave her a pointed look, her hand on her hip, though her lips still stretched into a smile.

Margaret covered her mouth as the tears slipped down her cheeks. All those times she had thought her sister was being lazy and petulant, she had been working through her grief in the only way she knew how. And now, she was gifting to Margaret the token which she had spent hours upon hours laboring over. Rising from the table, Margaret went to her sister and wrapped her in a tight hug, holding her close for quite some time as tears spilled down her cheeks. Then, with her face still tear-stained, Margaret glanced around the room at the women who had come to show their love for her.

"I dinnae know what I will do without all of ye."

"Ye will do just fine," Petunia said, though her wrinkles still revealed a smile.

Iain moved over to Margaret and wrapped an arm around her. Muireall nodded in his direction before she laid a hand on Margaret's stomach. "Ye will have Iain, an' ye will have this bairn."

"An' the good Lord," Petunia piped up again.

Margaret leaned into her husband as she wiped her tears away. Still, she was overwhelmed by the amount of love in that single, small room. More love than she had ever felt in her life.

Finally, Margaret clasped her hands together. "Time for food." She grinned as everyone congregated around the table.

Petunia had brought a venison stew, the recipe for which was in the journal she had given Margaret, as well as the one for the cinnamon apples Muireall had prepared. And Betty had brought more of her delicious bread, which Margaret was able to fully enjoy this time. Everyone dished up their food and dispersed around the cabin, with her and Iain on the bed,

Muireall and Betty at the table, and Petunia in the tiny rocker that fit her slight frame perfectly. Though the food was delicious, the company was even better as Margaret enjoyed one last night with her friends. The women all chatted easily. And when everyone's bellies were full, they helped Margaret pack. Despite the tears that dotted eyes, the room thrummed with energy.

Petunia was the first to retire for the afternoon, allowing the younger women some time alone. When Iain returned from walking her home, he confirmed that the rain had come to an end and the cloud cover was breaking. Besides a little mud, the next day would be perfect to begin their journey.

When dusk drew near, Betty returned home so she could prepare a meal for her husband. Margaret hugged her firmly, praying that somehow, she would be able to stay in touch with these women.

Sometime later, Muireall turned to her sister. "I suppose I need to head home an' check on Petunia."

Solemnly, Margaret nodded. She followed Muireall out into the evening, where only a splash of pink and purple remained in the sky. A chill had crept into the evening, and she wrapped her arms around herself as they stood together.

"Do be careful," Muireall reminded her once more.

She nodded and looked into her sister's pretty face, thankful for the health and love she found there. "Ye as well."

"Of course. Ye will be a wonderful mither, Margaret. I want ye to know that."

Tears rimmed the edges of Margaret's eyes again. "Thank ye. I am goin' to miss ye so much."

Muireall's face reddened in the dim light as her own tears welled. "An' I will miss ye."

They hugged and held each other for a long time. Margaret closed her eyes, trying to memorize the feel of her sister's embrace and not wanting her time with her to end. Finally, she pulled away.

She wiped at her tears. "I will be by to tell ye goodbye of a mornin'."

Muireall nodded and turned to leave. And though Margaret would see her again in the morning, she still felt as though she was leaving a piece of her heart behind.

~

Margaret shifted her weight, attempting to become comfortable on the bed of pine boughs and fur that her husband had so thoughtfully constructed for her. But one of the branches poked painfully in her middle, no matter how she laid. With her legs and her feet already aching and exhaustion overwhelming her, she could not help the tears that formed in her eyes. Not only did she long for a sleep that would not come, but she felt hopelessly alone. With the pine-bough bed only large enough for her, Iain slept several feet away. Margaret rolled her lips inward and pressed her mouth together to keep any sound from escaping as tears slipped down her cheeks. After her husband had worked so hard to make her comfortable, she could not let him know how miserable she was or how desperately she would rather lie on the hard ground alongside him.

She laid there for a while, allowing her tears to fall and hoping that eventually sleep would claim her. But it seemed it might elude her the entire night. Wiping at her face, she started to roll over once again. But then she could see Iain's handsome face through the darkness, and it reminded her of how uncomfortable and alone she was. A sob slipped out, and her hand flew to her mouth.

Iain had already awakened, though. Brows drawn together,

he sat up on his elbow to peer at her. Then, in an instant, he was by her side.

"Margaret, darlin', what is wrong?" Her circled his arms around her and pulled her close, his breath warm against her neck.

Margaret shook her head, still not wishing to reveal her displeasure with the sleeping arrangements. Instead, she nestled deeper into his embrace, resting her head on his chest with his chin atop her head. The warmth and comfort of him soothed the aches within her heart. There, she could have found rest. But his chest rumbled against her ear as he asked another question. "Are ye missin' Muireall already? If ye have changed yer mind, we can go back. It has only been a day."

Margaret closed her eyes as her tears continued to fall. But now a smile stretched her face and the tears had changed to happy ones. For she had the most thoughtful husband in all the world. After all the struggle and disagreement they had gone through regarding leaving the fort, after it nearly ripped their marriage apart, here he was offering to return for good, all to make her happy.

Margaret pulled back and put a hand to each side of his face so that she could admire him. "Ye are the most incredible man in the world. Ye are the one I am missin'. I cannae find a comfortable position to lie on the pine boughs, an' I miss ye lyin' beside me."

Iain chuckled. "Oh, darlin', ye can lie beside me all ye want." He leaned in and kissed her, his lips cold from the cool night air. But then he pulled back and looked her in the eye once more. "But ye are sure that is all? Yer not homesick for the fort? An' this is not too hard on ye?"

"Nay." Though her body ached and she was exhausted, she was still glad to be on the journey with Iain. The thought of making a life with him in that valley in Kentucky...of their child running through the grass beyond the cabin one day, it was enough to give her the energy to keep going. "I can handle the trip," she reassured him. "An' though I miss Muireall, ye are the one I want to be with."

He kissed her forehead. "Good. Then come here, an' let us try an' get some rest." There was a smile in his voice as he laid back down and brought her along with him, so that she was snuggled against his front.

Finally, wrapped in Iain's arms, Margaret found the comfort that had been eluding her. *Thank Ye, Lord.* She smiled as she curled up and closed her eyes, the warmth of her husband permeating the cool October night and dashing away the loneliness that had threatened her. As she settled in, sleep already tugged at her.

She'd not sleep anywhere but beside him for the rest of the trip. Despite how their marriage had begun or all they had gone through since, Iain had become her safe haven. With all her heart, she knew that their union was a blessing from God above. And as long as they kept the Lord at the center of their marriage, they could tackle any obstacle that was laid in their path.

CHAPTER 16

$\mathcal{A}$s the first settlement outside Pitman's Station came into view, Margaret breathed a sigh of relief. Not only did it signal that the majority of their journey was behind them, but that they would be blessed to sleep inside a warm cabin that night.

Though the first several days of their trip had been beautiful and comfortable, ideal weather for such a task, the rains had brought a crisp coolness to the air the day before. And now, after traveling the day in more misting rain, she could barely feel the fingers she kept curled into fists under her crossed arms. Iain had offered to allow them to remain another night until the rain had fully passed, but Margaret knew that one should only encamp in the same place multiple nights when of the utmost necessity. Iain had taught her that when they had journeyed to the fort to begin with. And after he had spotted signs of Indians in the area as they started out that morning, she was certainly glad they had chosen to move on.

She was also supremely grateful for her husband's foresight to make her fur cloak before their journey.

Still, that did not stop Margaret's nose from running or the cold from nipping deeper within her with each passing hour. Not to mention the fact that, though she remained strong for Iain's sake, every inch of her body ached from their travels. While her muscles had grown disappointingly weak living within the confines of the small fort, her blooming midsection added further strain as they journeyed mile upon mile uphill and down.

Iain came up beside her, Goldie trailing along his other side, and placed an arm around her shoulders. "Almost there, me darlin'."

Margaret nodded, though she kept her lips pressed together to prevent her teeth from chattering.

When they made it to Pitman's Station, she would dig some warmer clothing from their packs. It had been careless of her not to do so that morning, but she had been anxious to get on the way. And now, here they were, nearly to the station, with home a mere day's travel away. It energized her steps and kept her pressing on into the mist.

Finally, the scenery gave way to the fortified cabin that was Pitman's Station, with Sinking Creek bordering it on three sides. Margaret turned a smile to Iain, finally able to forget her chill. He squeezed her tighter before they approached and knocked on the heavy wooden door.

Sallie Pitman opened the door, her face friendly and a broad smile blooming as recognition dawned. "Welcome! Come in, come in." She held the door wide and ushered them in with a wave of her arm.

"Thank ye," Margaret whispered as she offered a smile.

"Go ahead and shed your wet layers, and we can lay them out to dry. I am sure you are chilled. 'Tis such a dreary day for travel." Sallie gently guided Margaret toward the crackling fire at the center of the large room.

"I should say so," William Pitman agreed as he descended

the wooden ladder from the second level of the cabin. "Donegal, I will come help you unload your mare."

Margaret turned to see her husband still lingering by the door. He gave her a quick wink before he and Mr. Pitman ducked back out into the rain. A smile curved her lips as she turned back to Sallie and the wonderful warmth of the fire. Shedding her cloak, she hung it on the back of a rocker and settled into the seat.

"You have dry clothes in your packs?" The other woman lifted her brows in inquiry.

"Aye." Margaret nodded as she soaked in the precious heat that drifted in her direction. She stretched her legs out as her hands and feet began to tingle.

"Good. We will have you all warmed up directly." Sallie patted her hand, her flesh warm against Margaret's, before she settled into the rocker across from her as they waited.

Moments later, both men walked in with their arms laden. Sallie gave Margaret use of the upstairs where they slept to change into dry garments, and within no time, she was rocking beside the flames once more, humming to the baby while Sallie Pitman prepared a rabbit stew for the evening meal. Finally warmed completely though, with her feet resting and tantalizing aromas drifting to her nose, she could not be more content.

∼

*I*ain attempted to focus on William Pitman's words, but it was difficult when his wife's enchanting voice drifted to him from where she rocked beside the fire, her eyes closed and one hand stroking her belly, seemingly without a care in the world. Not only was she a welcome distraction, but it warmed his insides to know that she was resting and content. Though Margaret did her best to conceal it, the journey was wearing her down. He could not have been more thankful for Pitman's Station to come into view, and for the knowledge that they were only a day's trip from home. His right foot began to bounce against the wood floor of the cabin, beneath the table where he and Pitman sat, as he considered carrying his wife over the threshold into their home.

"Did not take long for love to grow, did it?"

He whipped his head in Pitman's direction as the man's words registered. "Nay. It did not," he agreed before stealing another glance in Margaret's direction.

"Is that what brings you back? To make a home together here?"

Iain nodded. "Aye." A tiny niggle of guilt tugged at him, given the temptation that had nearly brought him and their marriage down. But, for once, he could rest easy knowing that was not why they retreated into the wilderness. For he and Margaret had taken their time and heeded the Lord's direction once Muireall was well. "Though her sister found her place there, the fort life was not for the two of us. God was callin' us back home."

"He does work in mysterious ways," Pitman confirmed. "I suppose some of us have to be called to this wilderness frontier."

Iain shrugged a shoulder as he chanced another glance at Margaret, who had fallen asleep in the rocking chair. While the Lord had indeed called them and written a story for them grander than anything he could ever imagine, the settlement of Kentucky was still a complicated subject. He held no wish to tame the frontier or encroach upon the Indians' homes. He only wished to find the place God had created for him and his wife.

A loud banging on the door brought Iain's attention around behind him. His brows lowered as he turned back to Pitman.

William stood and lifted the rifle that leaned against the

wall beside him. When more rapping came, he cautiously moved toward the door and pulled it open, his rifle held where he could easily use it.

"About time someone answered," a gruff voice said from the other side. "Is this Pitman Station?"

"Yes. And you are…?"

The newcomer harrumphed. "A body seekin' shelter from this relentless rain. We are a'travelin' west to where we aim to settle."

Pitman was quiet for a moment before he motioned the man in. A woman, likely near Muireall's age but with flaming auburn hair, followed him. Both were laden with supplies that they dumped to the right of the door. Pitman lowered his rifle as he closed the door, then held out a hand to the burly man who had entered his home. "William Pitman."

"Dugan Eliott." The man took Pitman's smaller hand into his broad one for a firm shake, though his face still revealed no pleasure in the greeting.

Pitman tipped his head to indicate for Iain to follow as he escorted the newcomers to the fireside. Iain stood and he and Pitman carried the straight-back chairs they had been sitting in over near the flames. Margaret sat up straight in her rocker, her eyes wide and blinking.

Iain neared Eliott. Not only was the man much broader and thicker than he, but he was also taller. Under his bright red-orange beard, his jaw was set as he turned a critical eye on the others in the room, taking them in each in turn. When Iain stood taller and met the man's gaze head-on, his eyes did not linger long. Instead, his disdain turned toward his daughter.

"Dinnae be rude. Have a seat." His brows lowered a fraction as he motioned toward the empty rocker.

Iain's brow furrowed at the man's callous treatment of his own daughter. He moved to stand protectively by Margaret's rocker while Pitman took a seat in one of the straight-backed chairs.

"You said you plan to settle," Pitman began. "Do you plan to do so here in Kentucky?"

"Aye, I am pressin' toward James Skagg's Station near Big Brush Creek. I mean to settle there with what is left of me family." Mr. Eliott's mouth set into a line and he glared in the direction of his daughter, as though it were her fault that there were not more members to travel on.

What had happened? The room fell quiet as though no one was quite sure what to say. Mrs. Pitman stirred the stew, her own mouth tight while her husband glanced between her and the newcomers.

Iain frowned. It must be difficult on families such as the Pitman's, never knowing what kind of people might take refuge within their home.

Mrs. Pitman broke through his thoughts as she turned a watchful eye to Margaret. "I hope you do not mind me asking, but I noticed how you have been mothering that little bump at your middle. Are you with child?"

"Aye." Margaret grinned and nodded. A beautiful flush covered her face as she brought her hand to her growing belly.

Though she had obviously suspected, Mrs. Pitman still gave a gasp at the news. "Oh, how wonderful." Her grin stretched from ear to ear, crinkling the corners of her blue eyes.

"Ah, I told you. All in God's time." Mr. Pittman moved to clasp Iain on the shoulder.

"Aye," Iain agreed as he smiled down at his wife. He placed a hand on her shoulder, and she took it into hers, rubbing her thumb across his palm as she rested her cheek against the back. Warmth swirled in his middle at her gentle caress, making him grip her hand tighter.

What a wonder it was to be in love. To give in to the unknown and the risks, and bare your heart to another human being. Now that he and Margaret had been through their first trials and come out the other side stronger, he could not imagine another scenario.

Suddenly, a profound gratefulness surged in his heart for the fact that he had ever happened across her and Muireall. And that he had heeded the still, small voice within him that had kept him from venturing too far. For he could not imagine events happening another way. He did not even wish to picture a life in which this beautiful, enchanting woman never became his wife. God had proved once again that His path was better than any a person could envision on their own.

~

*M*r. Eliott's daughter washed the dishes while Margaret dried them. Though Sallie had put up a fuss, they had insisted she allow them to relieve her of the duty for the night. Now, the middle-aged woman sat in her rocking chair, mending a shirt while her son sat on the floor beside her, practicing his reading. Margaret smiled at the touching scene before she turned her attention back to the young woman at her side.

The girl scrubbed at an imaginary spot on an already-clean stew bowl. Could she be working out her frustration over her father's hostility? Margaret's heart squeezed, for the man had yet to even introduce his only kin.

"What is yer name, dear?"

"'Tis Keturah. Like in the Bible." Her posture straightened, and for a split second, her eyes blazed with pride. But then her gaze darted to her father, and she resumed her scrubbing as she continued. "But me father calls me Kate. In Gaelic, it is spelled *C-e-i-t*."

Margaret grinned. "Meanin' pure."

Keturah nodded and chanced another glance in her

father's direction. The large man was well-occupied as he inhabited the other rocker, a pipe in his mouth. Keturah's lips pulled into a thin line. "Me mither chose me name, but father was displeased with it being Hebrew an' insisted he call me the Gaelic name for short. He never once corrected her, but has never called me Keturah either." Finally, the younger woman finished scrubbing the bowl and handed it off to Margaret. Though tears glistened in her eyes, she held her chin high.

Margaret offered her a small smile before she gave her arm a squeeze. "Well, I believe Keturah is a strong, beautiful name. An' if I am not mistaken, Skagg's Station is less than a day's travel northwest of here. We are a day south of here, so we shan't live too far from one another."

Keturah tossed a brief grin in her direction before she continued over-scrubbing another bowl. Whether or not Keturah wanted a friend, Margaret had learned the importance of friendship, and it warmed her heart to know that Sallie Pitman and Keturah Eliott would both be living near enough to visit from time to time.

~

*M*argaret's ears tuned into the sound of crying. Opening her eyes to the dark cabin, she glanced around. Only able to make out outlines and general figures, she failed to locate the source of the sound immediately. However, as it continued, she crawled to her feet, dislodging herself from her husband's arm. Following the crying, she crept to the side of the hearth where she found Keturah, hunched beside the stone fireplace.

The girl jumped when she noticed Margaret's approach. Her eyes went wide, the whites becoming evident in the darkness. "I am so sorry to wake ye. I didna mean to." She stood and started to retreat to the front of the room from where her father's snores drifted, but Margaret put a hand on her arm.

"What is wrong?" She frowned lightly as she whispered the question.

Keturah waved a hand. "Nothin'."

She tried to retreat again, but Margaret closed her fingers around the young woman's wrist. Something was bothering the girl enough to make her cry, and she deserved someone to speak to rather than crying alone in the dark. Margaret knew all too well how that felt. "Come, sit an' talk."

The girl glanced toward her father's form and back again before she allowed Margaret to guide her to where she had been sitting. Still, she gave Margaret a tentative glance before she started talking. "I was just missin' me mither an' brother, is all."

"That is certainly not nothin'. How long has it been since they passed?"

Keturah's mouth worked, and tears glistened in her eyes. "On the journey out here." She glanced down to where her hands were folded in her lap.

"Oh. Yer grief is still fresh, then. Though it will take time, an' the grief will always stay with ye in ways, it will ease. I promise ye. I lost both my pa and ma last year."

"I dinnae know what to do without them. Pa blames me, an' I have no idea how we are to go on like this."

Margaret sucked in a breath. "Do ye mind me askin' what happened?"

"It was a river crossin'. There had been heavy rains the day before, an' the river was swollen an' churnin' somethin' fierce." Keturah shook her head, the terror of that day reflected in her eyes. "We should not have attempted the crossin', but Pa was set on us movin' forward. He had been determined nothin' would put us back even a day. He is so...difficult. I should not have, but I encouraged me ma, told her we would make it. But..." She squeezed her eyes shut and shook her head again as more tears slipped out. "She dinnae make it. Me brother went back in, to try an' save her, but the river swept them both away." Another sob tore from her throat, and she clapped a hand over her mouth.

Margaret moved forward to circle her in a hug.

"Now Pa is left with just me."

Margaret held the girl with tears in her own eyes. If only there was more she could do for one who had been through so much. "It is not yer fault," she whispered into the girl's hair. "An' ye are not alone."

Keturah pulled back and nodded as she wiped her tears away. "I know. God is always with me. It is just...He seems so far at the moment."

"I understand." Margaret squeezed the girl's hand. "But time will show He has a plan in all this. An' if ye draw close to Him, He will draw close to ye."

Keturah nodded.

"An' dinnae forgot what I told ye. I know neither of us will be able to make the trip often, but we will be close enough to be there for ye if ye ever need us."

Finally, the younger woman's face stretched into a smile as her posture straightened. "Thank ye, Margaret."

At that, Margaret scooted over next to her new friend and began to describe where their homestead was situated off of the Green River. Keturah listened intently, hope and determination in her eyes. What an added blessing God had given them both.

CHAPTER 17

"Good luck and God speed on your journey," Mr. Pitman told Mr. Eliott as he and his daughter reached the door.

The man had awakened at the crack of dawn, demanding that his daughter rise as well. Within the hour, the two were ready to depart from Pitman Station. Sallie had not even been able to convince them to stay long enough to have a bite to eat, despite the look of longing that had come over Keturah's face. Of course, she had not expressed any desire to stay and had wiped the look away as soon as her father had turned his attention to her.

Mr. Eliott simply grunted at Mr. Pitman's well wishes. "Come along, Kate," he muttered instead, though she was right on his heels.

She gave his back a quick, discreet glare at his dogged refusal to use her given name. Margaret's heart ached as the young woman gave one last look in her direction. Keturah held her head high, though, her face full of resolve. While it was clear the girl was strong-willed and capable, Margaret prayed the Lord would see her through and allow her to find her way without her father breaking that precious will.

Moving next to her husband, Margaret snuggled into his side as he put an arm around her shoulder. Dropping a kiss on top of her head, Iain hugged her to him. Their child would be showered with love.

With their other guests gone, Sallie turned to them and clasped her hands together. "Well, I believe we could use that bite to eat now. Would the two of you like some hearty porridge before we send you on your way?"

"That would be wonderful." Margaret gave her a grateful smile as hunger gnawed at her. Meals on the trail had been much less than those at the fort, and her body was already protesting. Though, on the frontier, it did not take long for one to appreciate a warm meal, even when not with child. Especially when someone else was doing the cooking. And though the thought of being home at the close of the day sent a thrill through her, she would savor the last moments alongside these friendly people. Especially considering she and her husband were about to enter into a relative solitude.

So, as Sallie stirred the food over the fire, Margaret rocked gently in the rocking chair as she asked the woman about herself.

"My mother and father both passed shortly after we were married," Sallie shared. She glanced toward the door the men had exited through when they went to tend to the animals. "William was my strong rock, reminding me that the Lord was with me and that I still had a full future to live for."

Margaret returned her smile. "'Tis wonderful to have someone to stand by ye in the good times an' bad."

"As long as ye keep God at the center of it, He will continue to bless that union in ways ye could never imagine." Sallie stopped long enough to point her ladle in Margaret's direction, earning a chuckle.

Margaret placed a hand at her middle as she grinned. "Aye. We have been witness to that already." She watched Sallie stir the porridge a while longer before a thought struck her. "What was it like, movin' out here an' startin' over with a small child?"

Sallie paused again as she shook her head and gave a small laugh. "Nerve-wracking, to say the least." She stared at the wall as though watching a memory. "It was difficult. The journey west and those early days as we built the station were the hardest, though. Now, the dangers have all become almost normal. I can actually breathe when John leaves these four walls. The most important thing to remember is just to always trust in the Lord."

"That we will." Margaret nodded. Though, sometimes, that was bound to be harder than others.

As if she had read her mind, Sallie gave her a knowing look. "Do not forget, we are here if ye need us. Only a day's journey away."

"True."

Though Sallie was several years her senior, she could see them becoming fast friends, given the opportunity. What a blessing to have a God-fearing couple so close. Maybe they could visit occasionally. And if their cabin did prove unsafe, she and Iain could possibly find happiness on a settlement outside the station. Though, when Margaret closed her eyes, she could not imagine their future anywhere besides the cabin in the valley.

When Iain came back inside, he had a broad grin for her. "We are all ready to go after we eat." As he came to stand beside the rocker, he dropped a kiss onto her cheek.

"Perfect."

Iain seemed as excited as she about making their home together at the cabin, and that energized her more than anything. To see him throw off the shackles of his past and embrace their future warmed her heart.

~

Margaret put a hand to her belly as she pressed up the hill. Iain slowed and wrapped a hand around her arm to help her. She smiled as she took slow, deep breaths of the cool October air. But when they topped the hill, she stopped and leaned into him to rest for a moment. She closed her eyes, focusing on the brush of the breeze across her cheek and the strength of the man beside her. But when she opened her eyes, she gasped.

Iain startled. "What?" As his rifle swung up level, he glanced around.

Margaret chuckled and placed a hand atop the barrel of the rifle to lower it. "I recognize this. We are almost home," she explained. As she grinned up at her husband, excitement surged through her, giving her the strength to go on. Suddenly, the journey did not seem so difficult.

"Come on," she cheered as she started down the hill, one hand still under her belly as she held the other up to steady herself.

Careful not to lose her balance and tumble headfirst, she hurried down the slope, crunching over fallen leaves and green grass. Then, with new vigor, she climbed the next rise. Iain caught up with her and kept a hand at her elbow. Goldie plodded along on his other side, laden down with their belongings, which included a substantial amount of food to aid them through the winter and seeds to plant in the spring. The excitement of it all pressed her forward, farther, higher up the rise. For she knew what lay ahead.

And finally, they were there. She sucked in a breath as she crested the ridge and took in the beautiful sight in the valley below. Surrounded by trees of gold, crimson, and cinnamon was home. The cabin that her father had built and in which she would make a life with her family. Joy bloomed within as she turned to look up at Iain. His blue eyes sparkled with the same happiness she felt within her soul and offered the same sweet promise of a coming spring.

And just as it had on that morning on the mountaintop with her father, freedom seemed to surround them and envelop them. A world of opportunity lay before them, and anything was possible. For her, Iain, and their little one, this was only the beginning.

A sudden sensation in her middle took her breath. Iain's gaze turned to one of concern as she glanced at her stomach, putting a hand to the place she had felt the movement. Again, the feeling came. But this time, there was no mistaking the tiny kick against her hand. Her mouth opened wide, and she turned to Iain. "The baby is kicking."

Iain's eyes rounded and his lips parted. He slipped his hand atop hers, and she moved hers over his to allow him to feel the precious gift. When the child kicked again, a pleased and astonished chuckle emanated from them both. It was the most incredible sensation that Margaret had ever experienced. And to think that less than six months prior, she had not even known the handsome man beside her, the father of the tiny miracle God had created within her.

≈

*A*s soon as Iain was able to pry himself away from the miracle of feeling his child moving within his wife's belly, he took her hand and led her down the hillside to the cabin. Leaves crunched underfoot, signaling the coming fall, but bright, uplifting sunlight filtered through ginger-colored leaves overhead. The world was closing one season and opening another, a concept he could certainly relate to, having finally put his past behind him. Excited energy pulsed through his chest and spread onto his face in the form of a broad grin as he and his wife made their descent.

Margaret's own bright smile carried all the joyful innocence of a child as she glanced up at him. And when at last they made it into the valley before the cabin, she let go of his hand and spun around, her arms outstretched. She took a deep breath and expelled it as she came to a stop and smiled in his direction. "We are home."

Iain could not help the mischievous thought that quirked the side of his mouth as he drew near and caught his hand around her waist, pulling her close. "We are," he agreed, his voice husky as he brought her in for a kiss, one full of all the promise the day held.

Margaret pulled back and looked up at him admiringly. "I could not be happier to be here with ye."

"Nor I." He captured one more sweet kiss before he allowed the horse to graze and swept his wife up into his arms, which elicited a girlish squeal from Margaret.

"What are ye doin'?"

"Carryin' ye over the threshold, Mrs. Donegal."

Margaret blushed and grinned before he mounted the porch and shoved the door open. Stepping inside, they were not only entering their cabin, but a whole new life together. One blessed with love.

Did you enjoy this book? We hope so!
Would you take a quick minute to leave a review where you purchased the book?
It doesn't have to be long. Just a sentence or two telling what you liked about the story!

Receive a FREE ebook and get updates when new Wild Heart books release: https://wildheartbooks.org/newsletter

Don't miss the next book in the Frontier Hearts Series!

Reverence in the Wilderness
By Andrea Byrd
Releasing February 13th, 2024!

ABOUT THE AUTHOR

Andrea Byrd is a Christian wife and mom located in rural Kentucky, who loves to spend time with her family in the great outdoors, one with nature. Often described as having been born outside her time, she has a deep affinity for an old-fashioned, natural lifestyle.

With a degree in Equine Health & Rehabilitation gathering dust and a full-time job tethering her to a desk eight hours a day, Andrea decided it was time to show both herself and her children that it is truly possible to make your dreams come true. Now with over 1,000 contemporary Christian romance novellas sold, Andrea is pursuing her passion of writing faith-filled romance woven with a thread of true history.

AUTHOR'S NOTE

Thank you for joining me for the second installment of the Frontier Hearts series. I hope you enjoyed Margaret and Iain's story. This story combined the quiet Iain Donegal's story with an idea that had come to me long ago. Then, it was infused with some of my own ancestry as well as the colorful history of the beautiful state in which I live.

Pitman's Station as well as the briefly mentioned James Skagg's Station were both real fortified settlements in Green County, Kentucky. And though they have been fictionalized, William and Sallie were the real couple that founded Pitman's Station, and they did have a son named John. Another fictionalized but real couple present in this novel is that of James and Ann Harrod. James Harrod was the actual founder of both Harrodstown, which would become Harrodsburg, Kentucky, and Fort Harrod. In fact, you can still visit a replica of Fort Harrod today at Old Fort Harrod State Park.

If you enjoyed this book and wish to learn more about my writing, please join my Facebook reader's group, The Reader's Nest, where all lovers of Christ-centered romance can find a home.

You can find it at:
https://www.facebook.com/groups/374798130264410/

If you love historical romance, check out the other Wild Heart books!

The Pirate's Purchase by Elva Cobb Martin

Escaping to the New World is her only option...Rescuing her will wrap the chains of the Inquisition around his neck.

Marisol Valentin flees Spain after murdering the nobleman who molested her. She ends up for sale on the indentured servants' block at Charles Town harbor—dirty, angry, and with child. Her hopes are shattered, but she must find a refuge for herself and the child she carries. Can this new land offer her the grace, love, and security she craves? Or must she escape again to her only living relative in Cartagena?

Captain Ethan Becket, once a Charles Town minister, now sails the seas as a privateer, grieving his deceased wife. But when he takes captive a ship full of indentured servants, he's intrigued by the woman whose manners seem much more refined than the average Spanish serving girl. Perfect to become governess for his young son. But when he sets out on a quest to find his captured sister, said to be in Cartagena, little does he expect his new Spanish governess to stow away on his ship with her six-month-old son. Yet her offer of help to free his sister is too tempting to pass up. And her beauty, both inside and out, is too attractive for his heart to protect itself against—until he learns she is a wanted murderess.

As their paths intertwine on a journey filled with danger, intrigue, and romance, only love and the grace of God can overcome the past and ignite a new beginning for Marisol and Ethan.

~

Rocky Mountain Redemption by Lisa J. Flickinger

A Rocky Mountain logging camp may be just the place to find herself.

To escape the devastation caused by the breaking of her wedding engagement, Isabelle Franklin joins her aunt in the

Rocky Mountains to feed a camp of lumberjacks cutting on the slopes of Cougar Ridge. If only she could out run the lingering nightmares.

Charles Bailey, camp foreman and Stony Creek's itinerant pastor, develops a reputation to match his new nickname — Preach. However, an inner battle ensues when the details of his rough history threaten to overcome the beliefs of his young faith.

Amid the hazards of camp life, the unlikely friendship growing between the two surprises Isabelle. She's drawn to Preach's brute strength and gentle nature as he leads the ragtag crew toiling for Pollitt's Lumber. But when the ghosts from her past return to haunt her, the choices she will make change the course of her life forever—and that of the man she's come to love.

~

Lone Star Ranger by Renae Brumbaugh Green

Elizabeth Covington will get her man.

And she has just a week to prove her brother isn't the murderer Texas Ranger Rett Smith accuses him of being. She'll show the good-looking lawman he's wrong, even if it means setting out on a risky race across Texas to catch the real killer.

Rett doesn't want to convict an innocent man. But he can't let the Boston beauty sway his senses to set a guilty man free. When Elizabeth follows him on a dangerous trek, the Ranger vows to keep her safe. But who will protect him from the woman whose conviction and courage leave him doubting everything—even his heart?

www.ingramcontent.com/pod-product-compliance
Lightning Source LLC
Chambersburg PA
CBHW070315190726
48291CB00013B/1390